E- MAIL FROM AFRICA

A modern epistolary novel

AF175623

Catalina Onda

E-MAIL FROM AFRICA

A modern epistolary novel

Bibliographische Information der Deutschen Nationalbibliothek:
Die Deutsche Nationalbibliothek verzeichnet diese Publikation in
der Deutschen Nationalbibliographie; detaillierte bibliographische Daten sind im Internet über http://dnb.d-nb.de abrufbar.

2020 ONDA CATALINA
Herstellung und Verlag:
BoD - Books on Demand, Norderstedt
ISBN: 9783752609547

Name: *Stephen*
Current location: *Accra / Ghana*
About me:
I'm honest and trustworthy, down to earth and a good listener
Requests:
Looking for genuine, reliable, long-term friendship
Hobbies & interests:
Listening to music, reading, cultural exchange, online friends, my dog

Name: *Linda*
Current location: *Vienna /Austria*
About me: *Just find out!!*
Requests:
Interesting people from all over the world who really enjoy exchanging thoughts and experiences
Hobbies & interests:
Writing poetry, painting, plants, travelling, my little dog

13th of July 2011
Hello Linda,

This is Stephen from Ghana. Really liked your profile and would love to get in touch with you.

As for me, I'm basically fine, just as a single parent I sometimes feel a bit lonely. So I'm looking for reliable friends that I can share my life with, even if it be from a distance.
I have three children but I own only two, a boy and a girl. David is twelve and he likes music. My only daughter Mary is ten by now and she is truly daddy's little girl. I can honestly say that she and my little dog Penny are my daily joy. My ex-wife owns our oldest son John, aged sixteen, and my relationship with both of them is still quite complicated.

How about you? Have you got any children?
I have to confess that at first I always feel a bit inhibited about asking personal questions. On one hand I don't wish to appear nosy, but on the other hand I am aware that if I don't ask, it could also be interpreted as a lack of interest …

You know, it happens so often here on this webpage that people chat with you one day, and you actually enjoy a very nice conversation, but then you never hear from them again …

I would like to find a few honest friends from all over the world to build up significant long term friendships.

It bothers me so much when I see that many users have settings that block messages from African countries. Believe me, not everyone from Africa is a scammer! I am definitely not! I am a hardworking man from Accra, holding a job in a local hospital. I love my work, even though I don't like the pay so much. But I get by. Sometimes there are extra jobs at the weekend in private hospitals. Those are well paid and I can even save some money at times.

Well, my potential friend from Austria, I wish you a wonderful day!

Hope to hear from you soon.

Yours,
Stephen

14th of July 2011
Dear Stephen,

I really enjoyed reading your mail! And I love African countries! ☺

You mention that you "own" two of your children. Funny way to express that! ☺ Do you just mean that they live with you?

… By the way, my daughter Lori is also interested in music. She's got the possibility to do music at school for free as part of the regular school programme. She plays several instruments, and she's also twelve. Her sister Kate is fourteen and prefers sports. I also have four grown-up children who don't live at home anymore. The father of my first two kids was a Spanish intellectual, but later I married a man from Vienna. With my oldest daughter I have no contact. My only son is already married. He is a computer expert and enjoys making music with his own band. My daughter Clarissa is doing the most amazing acrobatics and fire shows. Alicia still attends a business college, but her love is singing, I guess. Besides, we also have a small dog, named Cora. I send you a picture of her.
Would you mind sharing a photo of Penny?

As for me, I teach German and English privately to make a living, but I'm a painter and a writer of poetry as well.

I don't know so much about Africa, and about Ghana I actually know nothing at all. I originally joined this platform because I wanted to find

11

someone to practice Swahili with (that's a language spoken in Kenya and Tanzania).

But in the meantime I got so many interesting mails from people all over the world that I decided to get myself a circle of international friends. I just love far away countries, and if I could handle it financially, I think, I'd visit every country in the world at least once. But unfortunately travelling is a very expensive hobby these days.

How about you?

(By the way, my Viennese husband and I separated long ago)
Linda

15th of July 2011
Hi, Linda,

So good to hear from you again! I can't believe how sweet Cora is! Lovely picture! What kind of race is this?

As for Penny, she is of mixed race, and I hope I can breed with her as soon as she is old enough. This can be good business here in Ghana because you can sell a puppy for about 350 Dollars. Well, you also have to pay for the male to get her pregnant, and that costs about 300 Dollars; but if she gets four puppies you can still count on quite a good profit.

Due to the fact that our money buys nothing abroad, international travelling is out of my reach. But I plan a journey to the north of Ghana next year. This has been a dream of mine for a long time, and I think the moment will come soon. I've heard that there is a lake with half-wild crocodiles!! They actually come out of the water, and one can pet them and take pictures!!
I really long to see this …

Referring to my words "I own two of my children" … In my African language we would use an expression that could best be translated with "own", when talking about child custody. Might not be the "correct" term in English, but I think it explains spot on the responsibilities involved. Like housing, feeding, medical care, education and discipline. It's your obligation to care properly for whatever you own!

What countries have you travelled to?
And how did you get Cora?

Sleep well, my friend!
Yours,
Stephen

16th of July 2011
Hi, Stephen,

Oh, I travelled to quite a few countries. I especially liked Sri Lanka, Cuba, Venezuela and Kenya.

Thanks for the pictures of Penny and your family. Penny is a cute little darling, and your son's quite a handsome fellow.
Please understand that I don't wish to send pictures of my kids to people I haven't met in person or known for a very long time because I feel this would violate the privacy rights of my children.

Cora is also of mixed breed, and it is not sure what all might be mingled inside of her.
It all started when our hamster died. Lori was just so heartbroken, and the very next day she had to go on a summer camp. That day I talked to her sister Kate and found out that she also loves dogs. This was new to me since she had never mentioned it before. Lori, on the other hand, had already asked me quite a few times, and I had always explained to her in detail why having a dog was too big a responsibility for me.
But, considering the fact that there would be three of us to take care of the animal, I started to seriously think about it, and I also had in mind

that this could be a joint project to unite us more as a family …

So I searched the internet a bit and instantly got in contact with all kinds of people who offered so-called "mini dogs". Since I do not fancy dogs myself, I had the idea that it should be as small a dog as possible. Just for fun we went that night to a place where they offered Chihuahuas. They were little, but I don't know… They somehow didn't touch our heart. Next, we still went to another family's home where they also offered a "Chihuahua" which looked quite different from the ones we had seen before.

As we entered, the woman ordered the handymen to stop drilling. She proudly showed us a huge aquarium for turtles which was still under construction.

Then she explained that the dog we had seen in the advert had already been sold, but that she still had this puppy's sister. She grabbed the creature from the transport box under the table and swiftly placed it into my daughter's arms. "Still very little and cute", she said. "Sold with chip and passport. Vaccinations and worm treatment also included. Won't get bigger than one and a half kilos!"

The puppy snuggled up in Kate's arms.

"Oh mommy, how sweet! Look at this! I want this dog! Please, mommy!"

"Well, you know that we don't want to buy a dog now", I answered, "we have booked a holiday in winter and when we come back, then it will be a good time to pick up our little doggy. So, it should be born around the end of October or the beginning of November. This will give us some time to study up on how to take care of it. Besides, we should visit the puppy beforehand several times and get to know it step by step until we finally take it home … "

"But mommy, I want *this* dog! Look, it is here all alone and those people are not nice to it. They lock it inside a box and let it stand here, in this noisy place. The children in the other room don't even play with it! "

"Let me see!" I picked up the wee little something. It felt soft and had a wonderful "baby smell".

"Please, mommy!"

"Well", I said, "I agree that this dog is exceptionally sweet ... And if you are a hundred percent sure that it is *this* dog you want, then we would have to take it now because in four month this puppy will of course not be here anymore."

"I am sure, mommy! This is the right dog!"

Well, Stephen, the end of it was that we bought that puppy. The lady wrapped it into some old baby blanket and told us that it only liked very fresh water. As we left, Kate carried the puppy,

16

and I was handed an animal passport from Slovakia.

When we arrived home, it was already quite late, and we arranged our laundry basket for the little one right next to my daughter's bed.

The following day, I noticed to my surprise that this dog couldn't walk properly. It moved its little hind legs in a strange way and had a tendency to topple while it intended to get forward. At first I feared it might have a paralysed leg, but luckily we found out some days later that our sweet one was just too weak to walk. My daughter named her Cora, and a few days later we took her to the veterinarian. There it turned out that she had no chip and that her passport was a forgery. Obviously she had never been to a vet before. We were also informed that the puppy's age of two month, according to documents, didn´t match its development and that it was probably no older than six weeks. Too young for legally crossing the border and in an age where it should still be with its mother!

You can imagine this was quite a shock!

At that time I didn't know anything about the fact that especially in the Eastern European countries there are many people breeding dogs under horrible conditions, just trying to make as much money on them as possible. It also turned out that this dog was definitely no Chihuahua.

The mother might have been a Chihuahua, but the father was probably a Yorkie or whatever.

Cora soon recovered, and after three weeks, when Lori came back from camp, she was already fit and fine. Since Kate had chosen and named the puppy, there wasn't much left for Lori, so I decided to proclaim the dog a "surprise". Yet, I was well aware that it was way too early for Lori to bond with a new animal. She still needed time to get over the loss of her hamster. Lori has a genuine intensity, and she is very loyal when it comes to love. She isn't the kind of person that would quickly replace one animal with another one.

Anyway, this was how we got Cora.

It would be interesting to hear how Penny entered your life! I'm sure you also have a story to tell!

Can't wait to hear it!

Take care,

Linda

17th of July 2011
My dearest Linda,

Wow!! What a story! I didn't know that such illegal things could happen in a civilized place like Europe.

Well, get ready to hear Penny's story:

Seven months ago, my former dog had an accident. Unfortunately there is a street crossing right through our property. In the past few years the cars got more and faster all the time, and by now it's getting somewhat dangerous.

Well, my dog Rex was hit by a car that didn´t even stop afterwards. Someone called me to come quickly, and I ran out to the dusty street where my poor dog was lying in a poodle of blood. I cradled him in my arms and we moved away from the street. I'll never forget the desperate look in his eyes while he whimpered with pain. There wasn't much I could do. I just held Rex close to my body until his eyes turned blank. I told him what a great dog he had been and how much I loved him. Then he died right there in my arms, and I was just so totally heartbroken and devastated. My eyes were blind with tears, and I just kneeled there on the barren ground next to the street for timeless moments, caught in a state of infinite grief.

Then, all of a sudden, there was this little boy who sat down next to me, his eyes filled with tears of sympathy. In his hands he had a tiny puppy, and he just quietly placed the little creature into my arms and insisted that I should keep it. This just touched my heart so much!! I could barely believe it …

Well, this is how Penny came into my life and she was very special from the start. You know, she is quite attached to humans! Most dogs in Accra, even if they have owners, prefer to be out in the street to fellowship with their own kind. Penny, on the other hand, loves to be at home. She prefers our comfy sofa to the porch, and she likes to sleep in bed with my son. She is also fond of human food, so we hardly ever buy any dogfood at all but rather share some chicken and rice or burgers with her. Whenever I come home, Penny runs to the door to welcome me, she jumps up and tries to lick my face, and she makes those excited squeaking noises … It's just so good to have her! Dogs can make you feel so immensely loved … I'm sure you know what I mean since you have Cora. She also seems to be very special. As I said before, some dogs are almost human. Maybe they are humans in disguise. But in so many ways they are practically better than humans, so maybe they are even angels in disguise. Who knows!

Well, my friend, I hope you have enjoyed hearing about Penny.

Looking forward to your next mail.
Yours,
Stephen

18th of July 2011
Dear Stephen,

What an amazing story! I can imagine that this must have been a very special day in your life, and I really feel with you …
Thanks for sharing this experience with me.
Say, why is there a road with heavy traffic crossing your property?
Sorry, but I don't have time to write more tonight. It's already late, and I am deadly tired.
Take care,
Linda

19th of July 2011
Dear Linda,

I was very happy that you still wrote a few lines before going to bed.
Well, let me try to explain why there is a road cutting right through our private estate.
Many years ago my father bought a nice piece of land here in Accra. In those days Accra was a lot smaller, and there were very few cars around. I still remember how our land looked when I was little. It was very green, and there were many old trees that gave us shade on hot days and delicious fruit in their due season. We had huge

mangoes, about the size of a small melon. When you cut them with a knife, there ran so much juice out of the fruit that you could fill half a glass with it. We also had mangosteen, coconut trees, and bananas. Our whole property looked like a tropical garden. Like a little paradise! The plants made the air feel so fresh and clean! At that time there were only four little cottages. In two of them my father and his brother lived, both with their families, the biggest house was inhabited by our grandparents, and the fourth unit my father had already built for one of his children. In those days when we all were still little, he could rent it out. This brought a welcome extra income for the family which of course could always be needed. As years moved on, the children got married, and more and more houses were built for all those new and rapidly growing families. Besides, some other relatives moved here, and in the meantime there are about 13 individual little houses right here on this piece of land. I couldn't tell you exactly how many people live there altogether, it's gotten a little bit out of hand. There are of course endless conflicts between all these families, each ruled by different parents who have all individual ideas and standards when it comes to housing or raising children and so on. My sister for example cultivated the most delicate and colourful flowers that really pleased the eye of everyone who passed by, yet when the kids of her cousin who lived next-doors grew old enough to play outside on their own, they always picked them, which resulted in a long-term conflict. In our cousin's opinion these "greens" were not that important, but my sister was emotionally attached to her flowers and definitely not willing to give in …

In the past some of us also tried to grow their own vegetables on a small patch next to their house, yet others wanted to keep a goat or some chicken. Now you can imagine that those animals often destroyed the fields of a neighbouring brother, which has all lead to endless arguments and fighting amongst the family members. As for myself I try to keep contacts to a minimum, but you always get involved somehow. There is hardly a day where I don't have a relative coming up to my house because he has some kind of a problem to sort out. And everybody calls for my support, of course. On one hand it feels nice to be respected by the family, and they do respect me, due to my job at the hospital, but on the other hand it drives me crazy. Sometimes I feel a very strong wish inside of me to live somewhere alone in complete peace and quiet. I don't know if you can understand me. It sounds so mean to talk in such a way about your family, and sometimes I feel bad about it.

Well, I have to get back to how we got the road. At the time when my father was already quite old, the property had changed dramatically. Trees had been removed to make room for more houses, and most of the land had become barren. At some point the state wanted to construct a major road right through our property as to connect the outskirts of Accra with the centre of town. At first my father proudly refused to sell the needed square metres, but in the end he allowed them to build that road because he was offered a nice piece of money for it, which, of course, came in hand. Around here you cannot expect to get anything like a pension that you could live on decently in old age, so you have to keep using opportunities that provide you with some extra cash.

So I hope this has answered your question. I' m actually feeling a bit sad right now. I have to admit that I miss the beauty that this piece of land had when I was a child. But well, Linda, times have changed …

By the way, how do you live?
Tell me about it!

I have to stop writing now.
Hope you are not so tired today.
Sweet dreams!
Your friend always,
Stephen

20th of July 2011
Dear Stephen,

It was interesting to hear about your family property. I found it strange that on one hand you all live so close together, but on the other hand you don't even know how many people there are.

Ok, since you have asked, I'll tell you something about my personal housing situation.
Four years ago I moved to the place where I live now. Before that I had lived for eleven years in a rented apartment, which had been a very complicated financial situation, due to huge housing bills. You have to know that exactly around the time when I separated from my husband, my mother got sick with breast cancer. Sad to say, she never recovered again and died after three years of treatment. At that point I had already five children, two of them in their teenage years and a baby. The flat in Vienna used up all the money I could earn, but suddenly I had to pay the bills for my mother's property in Spain too. Believe it or not, it took altogether eight years until the inheritance was finally settled. Unfortunately that year the rent for the flat in Vienna went up again, this time to a level which I definitely couldn't afford anymore. So, with good luck, I was able to sell my mother's house, and I bought a flat in Vienna instead. I was amazed

that this actually was possible at that time because my mother had moved to Spain during a period when prices there had been about half of Austrian standard. But as you already mentioned in your last mail, times had changed in the meantime, with the result that even a house in a run-down condition, like my mother's, could be sold profitably. So I felt tremendously lucky when I moved into my new place. Until the very end I was horribly afraid I might become victim of some kind of fraud. I knew that this was my only chance. I mean, the man who sold me the flat wanted to settle the whole deal in his brother's office since that sibling happened to be a lawyer. I was so extremely mistrustful. I even ordered that man to show me his valid licence. And then I asked him to show me the payslip that proved that he had paid the current bills of his insurance. He was quite surprised, as you can imagine …

And deep in my heart I was never sure that I would really receive the money from Spain on my bank account. I even said so when I signed the preliminary contract. I told them that I was a hundred percent willing to buy, but in case I had fallen victim to some fraud in Spain, I would have to resign because the profit from selling the house was my only possible way of financing this new flat. But all worked out fine. So around Easter I received the keys, and a few weeks later the purchase contract was settled.

From then on my situation improved greatly, since I didn't have to pay that high monthly rent anymore.

The flat is located in a house with four floors, and I live on the first one. All my windows face the south side, and I have flower-boxes in front of them. There I grow tomatoes and strawberries. This summer I have even planted a little fig tree and a kiwi plant, and due to excessive sunshine and lots of water, it looks like there will be a satisfying harvest.

And I just love my view: Right in front of the house you can see a beautiful old tree, and in the background there is a church with a park. The church tower strikes the clock, one strike for quarter past, two strikes for half past, three strikes for quarter to and finally four strikes when the hour is full. Then it changes the sound and indicates the hour by striking for example five times for five o' clock and so on. I hope I haven't explained this too long-winded.

This tree is very special to me. It was the first thing I saw of this flat because as soon as you open the door, your eye is directed to the windows, and in the windows you see that tree in all its beauty. And you can watch the whole cycle of nature because in winter one glance out of the window, even from my bed, can tell me if there is snow. It looks so magical at times! In winter you can also see all the branches in detail and marvel at the amazing built of such an ancient monument of nature. I have to say, that to me, trees are probably the most wonderful and advanced life-forms on earth. They are just strictly awesome …

To get back to *my* tree, in spring you can delight in the tender new green that will later change into mature foliage. And finally in fall, one gets to witness the changing colours of autumn that can fill our heart with excitement, even after all the flowers of summer are gone …

Oh, yes, and talking about plants, I also have to mention a place that I like to call "not my garden".

Well, I have to explain, there is a backyard that belongs to our building and when we first moved here it looked truly awful. Full of junk and rubbish. Seems, some people got new windows in the past and just didn't bother to clear away the broken glass that eventually fell down into the yard. There is a tree and a few hedges, and in some extended spots the grass fails to grow due to an obvious lack of light, whereas in other parts there is a huge patch of a seldom species of moss that stretches out like an asymmetrical carpet of almost artificial appearance. But as I learned later from a friend who happens to be a biologist, this highly resistant and evergreen moss might have well lived on the face of the earth since the last ice-age.

Anyway, I decided to adopt that little garden. First I cleaned it for many hours. I think, in the end there were about five kilos of broken glass and ten big black garbage bags, full of other waste material that had been left there to rot away quietly, probably for decades. Then I started to plant flowers but initially failed because there was not enough light in this dark yard. Later I found a solution to the problem. I left the plants in pots and placed them on the one end of the garden where at least some sunshine comes in. And as soon as the plants started to sprout blossoms, I moved them back to the deep shade where I actually wanted them. It turned out that the blossoms had a very long life that way since sun and heat make flowers flourish quickly.

In the end the garden looked beautiful. I put up a small table with chairs in a sheltered corner and placed a plastic pool with four goldfish right under the tree. I started hanging out in the yard, and sometimes other neighbours came down and marvelled. And people started to call this place "Linda's garden", to which I, of course, always replied that it was *not my garden*. Since actually it wasn't. It was everybody else's garden just as much as mine.

Oh, Stephen! I've totally forgotten the time while writing. I can't believe how long this mail has developed. Seems when I start writing to you, I just never run out of words. That's incredible!

I really have to stop now.
Hope to hear from you again soon.
Yours,
Linda

21st of July 2011
Hi, my wonderful friend,

What a beautiful mail! Thank you so much for sharing all those things with me. I could practically see and smell the flowers, the way you described them so vividly. I'm happy to hear that you are now living under such fortunate and fulfilling circumstances. You really deserve it after all those hard times you've gone through before.
"Not my garden" – what a creative expression; so playful. I wish we could sit there together now sharing some tea and a joyful conversation. It would be so nice. Actually I think this garden is truly yours – even if not your property – because things tend to become the belongings of the people who care for them.

Say, why were you so afraid when you sold your mother's house and bought one in Austria that you could be a victim of fraud? I've always thought in European countries the laws are very good and one can trust things to be handled legally. Not like in Africa where rich people can do whatever they want. Is this just an unexplainable fear of yours or do those trust issues derive from bad experiences you actually had or witnessed in your close surroundings? I would be interested to know, but if you feel, this question is too personal, just tell me so. I want you to be comfortable with our conversation.

Don't worry that your mails could get too long, I'll never get tired of reading them. I'm so glad that you don't just want to have a bit of shallow chatting here on this platform when you are bored, but that you actually exchange something meaningful and honest with me.

Really, Linda, by now you have become a very important person in my life and I never want to lose you again. This would be like falling back into a stage of utter darkness.

I hope I will always be worthy of the trust you show me.

Your true friend always,
Stephen

22nd of July 2011
My dear friend Stephen,

I'm afraid I'm going to destroy your illusions about Europe with this mail.

Well, talking about fraud when it comes to finding a flat, I've already had quite a few unpleasant experiences myself, even here in Vienna.

After I had moved out from my husband's place, I had at first a very small but well-kept apartment, which quickly became too small after the birth of my new baby. So, an intensive and time-consuming search for more adequate housing stretched out over the next few months.

The first promising offer came from a man, who had a flat to rent out in the same district. This guy was a real country-bumpkin. Already his dialect was so extreme that you automatically trusted him. He just seemed too simple a person to be a scammer. Yet, I was very cautious. And I guess something was fishy because all of a sudden he wanted to exchange keys for cash in a café instead of doing so directly in the flat. I refused and he just never called back again. Many weeks later I received a letter from him. He tried to encourage me to meet him in this place to have sex, mentioning that he had well noticed, how much time I had been taking to inspect the bed! (Well, I had looked at the bed indeed for a longer time because I was trying to estimate how many of my children could sleep in it.)

Some weeks later I ran across an ad, offering a three-room flat for an incredibly cheap price. This fact alone should have made me wary, I guess, but after having already seen quite a few flats and suffered one disappointment after the other, one just hopes that maybe one could finally land a lucky catch. Well, I went to see this lady, with my new born baby daughter along. She came to the appointed address with her two smaller kids, kind of building up trust from mother to mother – so to speak. After showing me around, she offered tea and cookies, and we had a nice chat about all kinds of stuff. Then we agreed to settle the deal. She presented me a contract that we filled in together and finally signed. It is the custom here to make some kind of a down payment at this point of the transaction, so I handed her the money, and she gave me the keys. I tried them out, and they matched the lock, so everything seemed to be correct. She just kindly asked me not to enter the flat before the first of January, claiming that her grown-up daughter was unable to move out before the end of the month. Of course, I agreed.

It was about ten days later when I heard about that very lady on the radio. She had fleeced quite a few people, signing them all contracts. That way she had collected multiple down payments.

Even though the woman's full name and address were mentioned in order to warn people, I still refused to believe it at first. After all I had the keys! I even still went to the place on the first of January and tried to get in. Of course, the lock had been changed in the meantime.

In that case I lost the equivalent of roughly 2000 euros which I never got back!

As for Spain, one always had to expect problems to come along with financial transactions. When my mother moved there, she wanted to buy a twin house but at that time they didn't have one ready. So she temporarily set up a household in half a twin house, waiting for the new units to get finished. When it was time to pay for the second duplex-half, the money miraculously disappeared! The bank in Germany where my mom had posted it from, confirmed that they had sent it, and also handed out a document in support. But the real estate office in Spain just asserted that they had unfortunately not received any cash transfer. So my mother had a problem. And to worry her even more, she heard all kinds of stories from other foreigners who had sent money from abroad; and the money had disappeared somewhere between banks and borders and never shown up again. In this case my Spanish husband

settled the problem. He knew his fellow coun-
trymen too well. After threatening the boss of the
bank in ways he knew would work, the money
magically turned up again within only two days.

The root of the whole action had probably been
the fact that Spain was about to join the European Union which caused the prices to skyrocket.
That way, the agency speculated, my mother
could be charged a much higher price. They just
insisted that the payment had unfortunately been
received after the deadline. And therefore the
new price needed to be applied.

Well, they didn't make the deal at all in the end,
because my mother's finances were tightly calcu-
lated, and she just wasn't able to pay any more.

Oh, Stephen, all this talk about fraud has kind of
exhausted me.

How is Penny?
Cora sends sweet doggy-greetings to her.

Take care,
Linda

23rd of July 2011
My dearest Linda,

Hard to believe for me what you told me in your last mail. You really expand my horizons. Such stories I've never heard about Europe so far. That's the good thing about getting first-hand information from a friend who actually lives there!

Penny also sends some greetings back. Too bad they can't play together. I'm sure they would have a lot of fun.
Tomorrow I start work early, so I might end up getting very little sleep tonight. To start at eight doesn't sound so bad, but it means getting up already at four in order to beat morning traffic into Accra. It's incredible how busy the streets are in the morning. Normally Africa is sparsely populated in most places, but this definitely isn't true for Accra. All these cars and bikes. All those pedestrians who block the streets, trying to sell you something. Luckily I have an old motorbike which enables me to get ahead in spots where the bus would be stuck for an hour. On the other hand, if you wish to buy some food, it's convenient to have everything readily available. Actually I love street food. It's usually well prepared and very fresh. I often get chicken or other deep-fried goodies with rice. Or "fufu", one of our

national dishes. It is usually made with cassava flour and served with groundnut soup. Yams and "pillapia" (a kind of fish) are also very popular. Kelewele is a popular snack of fried plantain which I love very much. Many people around here also order "tsofi", which consists of turkey tails; and if you have more of a sweet tooth you can always indulge in "koko", a Ghanian porridge that we enjoy at any time of the day. It's popular with children as well as with adults. We also have something that tastes similar to a doughnut. We call it "bofro". I mean, only the taste is similar to a doughnut not the shape. "Bofro" comes in round little balls.

What street food do you have in Austria?

Sleep well and sweet dreams!
Yours,
Stephen

24th of July 2011
Dear Stephen,

Hope I still catch you before you have to leave. Since you have to get up so horribly early, I really would enjoy leaving a few lines behind for you to read just before you have to go.

Well, Austrian street food exists, even though the variety seems to be a bit limited. There is something called "Würstelstand" where people can choose from all kinds of sausages that come with mustard and horseradish. This is something traditional and still commonly present nowadays. Another dish is called "Langos". It's some dough rolled out in a round flat shape and then deep-fried in oil. It is often seasoned with garlic. As far as I know, this is something traditionally Hungarian. Now there is also food available that originally comes from other countries, like "Kebab", which derives from Turkey. Besides, in winter, there are many "maroni-friers". They offer roasted chestnut and sometimes also potato-chips and "Kartoffelpuffer", a kind of potato burger. During the cold season and especially around Christmas people also enjoy having a drink of hot wine, usually seasoned with spices like cinnamon and cloves.

In summer ice-cream is probably the most popular street food. There are many different flavours and ice-cream is sold in fancy ice-cream-parlours as well as in cones or paper cups, so that you can take it with you to consume while strolling along the street. Some shops offer up to twenty different flavours!! Some of them are always available, and others are changed every day. So there is plenty of variety to choose from.

Street food in Austria isn't exactly cheap, so I have stopped consuming it too frequently. But I love ice-cream, especially from the saloon at Schwedenplatz. It's not so sweet and made with lots of fruit and natural ingredients.

I wish we could have some ice-cream there together …

Have a nice day!
Linda

25th of July 2011
Dear Linda,

So sweet of you to drop me those lines at that early time. You've really made my day by doing so.

It was interesting to hear that street-food is expensive in Austria because here in Ghana the food sold in the street by locals is the most inexpensive food you can get. Expensive is only the food in the supermarkets because most of it is imported, and those chains are run by international companies.

So where do Austrian people, who don't have so much money, buy food?

You really got me craving that ice-cream, and I'll gladly accept your invitation to Schwedenplatz. Can you send me pictures? We also have ice- cream here, but the only flavour available is vanilla. I also love it, and I often keep a whole package in the freezer. Even Penny sometimes gets a lick of it when it is hot.
Have a nice day too.

Your friend,
Stephen

26th of July 2011
Hi, Stephen,

Well, the cheapest food we can buy in Austria is found at shops which are called "discounters". They sell good quality stuff for a very reasonable price.

Hope you enjoy the pictures of the ice-cream. This is just to give you an idea what we are talking about.

I'll write more tonight.
Linda

27th of July 2011
Oh my god, Linda!

Those pictures have really blown my mind! Incredible! I can totally understand why you fancy that place. I think, I would become one of their best clients myself if I lived in Austria. Just imagine: You and I sitting there together sharing that huge composition of raspberry, blueberry and strawberry ice-cream decorated with mango, pineapple and fresh berries, topped with whipped cream and caramel. Yummy, yummy, that just sounds so delicious …

Linda, you have no idea how much I enjoy hearing from you almost every day. I think I'm slowly getting kind of hooked on you. I don't want to sound demanding by any means, and I hope not to scare you away by being too pushy.

I definitely don't want to irritate you in any way. I know, everyone has all kinds of experiences on such dating and friendship platforms, and I am well aware that a lot can go wrong. And yes, often such online friendships are also a kind of escapism.

One time for example I met an American lady called Sally. We quickly developed a very close friendship. She was very unusual and open-minded. That lady just popped into my existence, telling me the most interesting stories about

41

her life in California. To me, it sounded like a fairy tale. I think she had a very good and well-paid job. She sent me pictures of her house, and everything looked amazingly fancy. Well, anyway, at some point she even invited me to visit her in America. I told her this was not possible for me, due to the hard fact that a flight ticket is something completely out of my financial reach. And she reacted very sweet and understanding. Even offered to pay for my way. I felt a bit embarrassed about that, but she told me that it would be her pleasure. And that money didn't matter all that much.

So I saved some cash in order to buy myself a passport. I ordered a handwoven skirt in her favourite colours which I planned to offer her as a gift upon arrival. Next I arranged the necessary days off with my employer while my excitement grew from day to day.

And then, all of a sudden, after weeks of preparing for that journey and discussing details, she suddenly stopped writing to me. She never explained why. Just left me behind without a word. I couldn't believe it at first. Thought that something must have happened to her. Maybe an accident. But then I noticed that she was obviously exchanging mails with other people. I wrote to her and asked what had happened. She didn't reply. She just blocked me.

I was so shocked and felt so devastated in that moment. I have to admit that I secretly cried for quite a few weeks. My colleagues at work asked a lot of nosy questions since I had told them about Sally and my invitation to America. I felt so ashamed. Like a natural born loser. And I have to say, this experience has left a scar on my soul. I know that you are a very nice lady and a good friend, but all the time I am afraid, that maybe you will leave me some day, just like Sally did. I know that I shouldn't think that way, but somehow I can't help it. I have to ask for your forgiveness concerning that issue because you have never given me any reason to feel that way. Yet I just can't control my fear of losing you. As I have told you before, you really mean a lot to me by now, and I wish I could feel more relaxed about our growing friendship and just take pleasure in our rich conversation without allowing the dark shadows of the past to fall on it.

Linda, may I ask you a favour? Could you promise me that you will never leave me without telling me why? If you should ever come to the conclusion that I am not worthy of your friendship anymore, then please tell me so and give me at least a chance to work it out. I would never hurt you intentionally, but things can get between people sometimes. We all know that. We've lived long enough to experience our share of hurt, grieve and loss. Sometimes people really don't get along. Sometimes they develop in different directions. But often we are just faced with some kind of misunderstanding that could be sorted out if given a chance. It would make me feel so much better if you could give me that promise.

Right now I am afraid of your reaction. You are such a valuable person, you know. Please don't get mad at me.

Yours always,
Stephen

28th of July 2011
Dear Stephen,

Thank you for sharing your thoughts and feelings with me in such an honest and personal way.

I have a lot of trust issues myself, so for this reason I can totally understand you.

And I can definitively give you that promise: I will never leave without an explanation and if we should have to leave each other someday, I will never go without saying good-bye.

But let's stop talking about losing each other now because this will only make us feel sad.

I'm so happy to have you in my life. You are a good and loyal person, and I highly appreciate having you as a friend. And you are welcome to write to me about whatever you choose. In my opinion nothing is too big or too small to share it with a true friend. So whatever you wish to tell me, please feel free to do so. Tell me about your experiences, both, good and bad; or about your problems, both, big and small; let me know about your hidden hurt, and trust me with your secret dreams. And even though there are thousands of miles between us, I'll be there to listen. I'll be there to feel with you. Always.

Love,
Linda

29th of July 2011
Thank you so much, Linda,

Thank you for writing me such a beautiful letter. You are, of course, totally right with everything you said.

"Trust me with your dream"! What a beautiful way to express this!

Well, I will trust you today with my most secret dream. So secret that I haven't told anybody about it yet.

I've already shared with you about my family situation. About how I sometimes wish to have a place that is only for myself. Quiet enough that I can finally hear my own thoughts. A place where my true inspiration can come alive and where I can find peace for my restless, troubled soul. It would be so wonderful.

Now, as I told you, due to my jobs at the private hospital I am able to save some money at times. And with that money I have recently bought a piece of land in the outskirts of Accra. My dream is to have a small house for myself with a nice garden around it. Right now it is just a patch of barren soil, but someday, I dream, it could be a little paradise.

Whenever I have money left, I buy some con- struction materials and call some workers who are building this house for me, bit by bit. Some- times I am afraid I might never manage to get it finished, but I hope I will. The very thought of it keeps me going. You know, at times our burdens get too much and too many. And sometimes I feel like I can't take it anymore. Then I just think about my dream house and how lovely it will be some day. And then, in the most inappropriate situation, I suddenly smile. Others might wonder why. But that's my little secret.

And now you, my dearest Linda, know about it!

Say, what do you think about this project? Is it egoistic of me that I have such wishes? And do you think I could ever manage to get it finished? Sometimes I'm afraid that this dream might be too ambitious for someone like me. You know, I can only do it bit by bit. And I never know how long it will take until I can buy the next load of bricks. After all, I am poor. And sometimes I get a little impatient.

Hope to hear from you soon.
Yours,
Stephen

30th of July 2011
Dear Stephen,

First of all you should stop feeling egoistic just because you feel the honest need to possess a little house all for yourself. I personally can understand this very well. Of course, Europeans are much more individualised than Africans. So, people in your surroundings might not share this opinion. Still, don't let anyone else tell you about your needs. Only you know them!

Besides, I think you can feel very privileged that you are able to build your own house. So, stop feeling poor! According to European standards, I would never call you indigent. You are exactly what we consider middle class. I'd also like to point out that most people in my country do not live in their own house. They rent flats, and no matter how much they try to save, it will never be enough to build a house. So, already for that reason, you should not see yourself as an under-privileged person. After all, you have the possi-bility to make your dream come true! And there is nothing wrong with building your house bit by bit. That way you avoid building up debts. And I' m sure you will manage in due season.

Take care,
Linda

31st of July 2011
Hi Linda,

You are definitely right. There are much poorer people in my country, so I shouldn't complain.
Thanks for encouraging me so much concerning the dream house. I'll send you a picture of it. Hope you like it. You know, a normal house is not so expensive to construct here, only if you

wish to have a top floor, it gets complicated. A house in local style costs about 20.000 dollars. For me a lot of money, of course.

As for my house, the foundation is already finished, and now one can watch the walls grow rather quickly, which is quite satisfying. We'll see how far we can get with the new bricks. The most expensive will be the roof. You know, the carpenter has to come and make the wooden construction first, and then the tiles have to be fixed. Windows and a good door are also costly.

By the way, Linda, we haven't spoken about our free time yet. What do you do when you are not teaching?

See you,
Stephen

1st of August 2011
Dear Stephen,

Thanks for the picture of the dream house. I will be so excited to watch it grow. You've done a great job so far!

As for my free time, I actually don't have so much of it. But I like to spend time in "not my garden", and I have also started a little construction project in the cellar. Apart from teaching languages I am also a painter and a poet. In the past I had an art studio for a while, but it took me about an hour to reach it by public transport. So if I wanted to paint in the evening, I had to leave the children alone, in order to go there. And you know how it is. You never feel quite at ease when you don't know what is going on in your home. I always worry that something might happen during my absence. This again isn't exactly favourable for the free flow of my creativity. And it also costs a lot to finance a flat and a studio at the same time. But now I'm constructing a home for my paintings, downstairs in the basement of the house where I live. And actually I do it in a very similar way like you. Bit by bit. Since I don't have to pay this huge rent anymore, I can save some money every month, and with this I've started to improve the cellar. The first thing I did was the floor. Before, there was only the raw dusty soil, but now there are terracotta flag stones that can be kept clean easily. Then I painted the walls white. In addition, I ordered a big window that can be opened and closed properly which is important to increase the circulation of fresh air and to control humidity.

The next step will be to get warm water and a toilet. Then I can spend as much time as I please down there, and still, if the children need something, I'm in the same building and can show up in my flat at any moment. That way it's an ideal situation, and I'm very thankful that this opportunity has arisen. So I spend quite a lot of time on painting right now, and I've also started writing a novel about my mother's life. It's quite a challenge for me because I have never written anything that long and continuous yet.

Apart from this, I sometimes go to the cinema or enjoy a theatre production. I also love seeing an art exhibit or a presentation of poetry. I don't do any sports, but once a week I go swimming. However, since I want to save money for travelling, as I told you before, I limit my spending here in Vienna.

What do you do in your free time?

Take care,
Linda

2nd of August 2011
Hi, Linda,

Wow, very cool! But actually it was to be expected that a classy woman like you would be interested in art and literature. But I realise you are an artist yourself! I've just taken a look at the paintings you have posted here on this website, and I like them very much. You are a very talented lady! Why have you chosen to write a book about your mother's life? Did you have a good relationship?

I also don't do any sports. Guess, you and I don't need that. We have very active, energy consuming lives! But say, where can you go swimming in Vienna? It's not located by the sea, or is it? I'm a bit confused about that right now.

As you know, my time is limited, and I don't want to spend too much money just on going out by myself. I have to care for the two children I own. I have the secret dream house. I have the extra jobs which I do in my free time. That's enough for me. And I enjoy music. You know, I like to lie down comfortably on the couch with little Penny right next to me, and then I turn the music on really loud. That makes me somehow feel good, I don't know why.

Hugs,
Stephen

3rd of August 2011
Hi, Stephen,

Well, you are right. Vienna is not located by the sea. But there is the river "Old Danube" where you can go swimming. And in winter I go to an indoor swimming pool with sauna which feels great in cold weather. Sad to admit, I often miss my Spanish home when I'm here in Vienna. Well, I guess I haven't mentioned yet that I used to live in Spain for many years. It wasn`t just my mother, who had a property in the province of Valencia, originally I moved there since my first husband was a Spaniard. In reaction to this, my mother relocated, so as to live closer to her family. But then, after some years, I separated from this man, with the result that my mother ended up in Spain while I was back in Austria again. Life can be a little crazy sometimes. You have to know, my mother was practically forced to stay there because she couldn't afford living costs in Austria anymore. At first her plan had been to have two homes in Spain, one for herself and one for renting it out. She expected this would bring her enough money to live on, and in the beginning it did. But some years later, it wasn't so easy anymore to find tenants for an apartment that wasn't exactly meeting modern standards. As a consequence, this second flat by the beach was mostly used by my family, and we continued spending a lot of time there until the children started school. Then we were forced to get a bit more sedentary. But I often miss my Spanish home, especially the way it was in the past. You know, Spain has changed a lot in the recent twenty years, and not all of this change was necessarily for the better. I still like it there, but unfortunately I can spend very little time in that place now. That's the way it goes. If you have a job, you are bound to live in the place where your job is located.

So I envy you a little bit because you can always live by the sea.

Do you have nice beaches in Accra?

I have to sleep now. So let's leave talking about my mother for some other day.

Bye,

Linda

4th of August 2011

Oh, Linda,

I'm afraid, this time I will have to destroy your illusions about Accra and the beach. Believe it or not, I cannot even swim.

Our property is located quite far away from the beach, and as a child I never happened to leave the area where we lived. There was no water anywhere near our place, no river, no lake, not even a pond. So there was no chance for me and my siblings to learn how to swim as long as we were little, and I guess once you have grown up you cannot learn it properly anymore. I mean, I can swim a little bit, but I never feel secure or any relaxed about it.

Talking about our beaches:

Well, we have a beach that is located right next to a slum. You see lots of people hang out there but they all come from this poor neighbourhood, so it's a bit dangerous. I mean, I'm not afraid to take a walk there, I'm a big, strong guy, but taking a swim would be a different issue. For swimming you have to take off your clothes and leave your belongings outside of the water while you enjoy your swim. And I can assure you that your valuables won't be here anymore by the time you come back. Even your clothes and shoes might get stolen. So, it's definitely not a place where you can spend a relaxing afternoon at the beach for people like you and me.

On the other hand, there is a beach on the other end of town where you have to pay. And the pay is something like ten dollars a person. Now imagine a family of four people going there spending forty dollars just for entering that beach! Then you can still get yourself a locker for your stuff, but for this you will have to pay extra. So this beach is definitely just for rich people.

I'm sorry to hear how much you miss your Spanish home. Sounds like you were very happy there in the past. We always miss the places where we have collected a rich measure of memorable moments. We always do.
I have to leave for work now.
Yours,
Stephen

5th of August 2011
Dear Stephen,

What a story! It's hard to imagine for me that people living in a town that is located by the sea cannot swim.
What a situation! For the one beach you are too poor, and for the other one you are too rich. This goes to prove what I have said before: You are middle class. And obviously your country has no setup for middle class people.
Don't feel bad because you can't swim. Reading your mail I remembered a little story my mother told me long ago. She also grew up in an area without any lakes or ponds, and her parents both couldn't swim. Nevertheless, her father success-

56

fully engaged in teaching both of his children how to swim. He organised a spare tyre from a friend's car as a swimming aid, and my mother and her brother actually learned how to swim in the river "Vltava". He could give them very professional advice about how to move the arms and legs properly because in theory he knew it all. He just never managed to swim himself. But he took pride in the fact that his children managed to do so. Well, I guess we always want our children to surpass our limits. ☺

As for my mother, I have to say that we had a very difficult relationship. I'm well aware of the fact that she had a complicated life. She grew up during the Second World War. At the age of twenty-seven she was divorced and alone with me. She always felt somewhat ashamed to be a single mother. And even though she had the constant help of my grandmother for anything related to household tasks and childcare, it remains a fact that my existence limited her to that modest village where I spent my early childhood. I know that her dream had been something bigger. A career, somewhere in the city. Or an intellectual husband. But under the given circumstances, she was bound to live with me in my grandmother's place, and I have to say that she and my grandma had a very quarrelsome relationship. Later, at almost forty years of age, she found the love of her life. Just that this man unfortunately happened to be married. Ten years later his wife died, and after a traditional one year period of mourning, they married. But only a year later they already broke up again. My mother couldn't deal with that disappointment. She eventually developed cancer in the course of some depressing years that followed. She tried to pull out of her depression by moving to Spain. But exactly then, when she got cancer, she had no health insurance. So she waited way too long before she started treatment, and by then it was already too late. After three years of therapy she died.

It was never easy to be her daughter. Only in those last years, when she had cancer, I finally came to respect her. In the end, even to admire her. Somehow, as often happens with people who have a life-threatening disease, her values changed. All of a sudden it didn't matter anymore what the neighbours thought. You know, I'd seriously wish I had the freedom of mind she experienced in those last years. Without having cancer, of course.

Writing this book about her is a possibility to put my thoughts and memories in order. And my feelings as well.

How about your parents? Are they still alive?
Bye for now,
Linda

6th of August 2011
Oh, Linda,

So sorry to hear about your mother. But again good to hear that in the end she finally found her peace and her true self.

As for my parents they have also gone to be with the Lord. My dear mother died in one of those lethal car accidents which happened frequently in former days. I was quite little at that time and therefore I can hardly remember her. My father also passed away, many years ago. I don't know if he had a disease. Maybe his body was just used up after all those years of heavy overstrain. The person I remember most was my father's sister who took care of me and my siblings for a long time. She also lived here with us on the property, and her house was next to mine. To me it was beyond question to take care of her in old age. But sometimes I would have appreciated a bit of help from my brother's side. Believe it or not, even on the day when she died, my brother showed no respect. He just invited a few booze buddies, and they got drunk. Last my brother ordered a prostitute, and you could hear their lustful screams and moaning right next to the cottage where our dear aunt was lying on her death-bed. Even during the preacher's holy ceremony, when he gave our dear aunty the last sacraments, we had to listen to those obscene and indecent sounds. It was utterly embarrassing.

That's one of the things I could never forgive my brother for. There are certain things that you just can't do. Under no circumstances. Some behaviour just cannot be excused.

My brother is no good. He's just a drunkard! Someday he will suffer the consequences of his evil life …

I'm sorry if I sound hateful, but the memories of that day make me feel utterly spiteful, even though I know that the bible says we should forgive.

What do you think about this story?

Yours,
Stephen

7th of August 2011
My dear Stephen,

Thanks for your kind words about my mother.

I can imagine that you must have been very disappointed about your brother's behaviour.

Actually, now I can understand even more why you long to get away from the family clan. It makes so much sense. Long live the dream house! ☺

Sad to hear about your parents' and your aunt's death.

But why did so many people die of car accidents in the past? I mean, at a time when there were actually very few cars around, and when speed used to be very slow compared to nowadays, how could such fatal accidents happen?

Yours,
Linda

8th of August 2011
My dear Linda,

Oh yes, accidents were common around here in those early days of motorised vehicles.

It wasn't about speed. It was about safety. There were no rules and no precaution. And most of all the roads were dangerously unsafe, especially during our rainy season. Wet roads are slippery and tyres often were old and didn't have enough grip. And drivers usually lacked experience. In my mother's case the car was going from one village to another. They were late for the market so they didn't stop when it started to rain. A small mountain needed to be crossed, and the road was slippery. When the car skidded, there was little chance to stop it in time. There was no guard railing alongside the road, not even on the side where the muddy slopes went down steeply. You couldn't survive such a crash. No chance at all. My mother didn't want to miss out on selling some hand-woven baskets there that day, just because of the rain. And then, due to that accident, she lost the rest of her life.

We cannot change it anymore, Linda. We just have to be aware what a precious and fragile thing life is and make the most of it. And be thankful for every day. For every moment of joy. For everything we have and love.
And Linda, I *am* thankful. Thankful for my children. For my work and for my dream house. And I'm extremely thankful that you are in my life.
Love, always,
Stephen

9th of August 2011
Oh, Stephen,

Thanks for explaining.

You are so right. We have to be thankful. Always. There is always something we should be thankful for. But sometimes we don't see it. We take things for granted. And yet we know that we have no guarantees for tomorrow. Your mother didn't want to delay selling her baskets but ended up losing the rest of her life. How true! My mother chose not to spend money on medical insurance. Always saving for future days. And in the end those days never came. It's all so grotesque! You know, I still have a hard time accepting certain facts. I've always been aware of the sad reality that in so-called developing countries there are people who have to die, just because they can't afford medical treatment. But it is shocking to me that a story like my mother's could actually happen right here in Austria, in a European Union nation that is considered one of the most social countries in the world. People from all over the globe aim to come here in order to profit from our outstanding social services. Normally everybody has medical insurance here. Also people who are unemployed or living on public aid. But my mother had seen better days in her life, and she refused to admit that she was suddenly poor in her older years. She still possessed a house, and in order to receive public aid she would have had to sell everything she owned and spend the money first, before our state would have supported her. Of course, she didn't want to do that. So she lived way below what is considered minimum income here, just to keep together what had taken her a lifetime to build up. For her it was a matter of dignity. Besides, Austrian government requires for people who want public money to live here in Austria where rents and housing are expensive. Well, my mother took a look at what kind of flat she could afford here in Vienna. After having seen quite a few bleak and depressing places where no sunlight ever entered the rooms and where horrible noise from the street made it little desirable to open the window, she finally came to the conclusion that she couldn't accept living like that. She stated in that dark humour she had developed in her last years that seeing how she could live here in Austria she'd rather die in Spain where at least everything that surrounded her was beautiful and made her feel at ease. I loved and admired that final consequence of her attitude. In my opinion that's character! But still, she lost her life because of this. And all those years before, she secretly suffered hunger! You know, she just came up with all kinds of excuses to make her situation sound normal to other people. Her neighbours usually assumed that she had chosen for a simple life, out of some love for simplicity or some eccentric rejection of materialism, but this was not the case. Yet, nobody would have guessed how serious and drastic her situation really was. I remember one time when I visited her, and she had actually marks on her loaf of bread indicating

64

how much she could eat every day in order to make that loaf last her for a whole week. She lost lots of weight to the point where she became dangerously skinny. She admitted that at times she suffered from dizzy spells but blamed it on the weather. She proudly told me about all kinds of cheap cooking recipes she had discovered by experiment. They all had in common that they used as little ingredients as possible. Altogether it was more the illusion of food than a nourishing meal. Totally absurd and crazy. And all of this took place in a social context where working class families nowadays definitely take it for granted to have at least food in abundance. In a country where even beggars tend to be over-weight.

Sorry if I sound bitter, but just thinking about it still upsets me a lot. I would have loved to help her more, but at that time I was a married housewife with no income of my own.

Yours,
Linda

10th of August 2011
Dear Linda,

While reading your lines quite a few memories flooded my mind. I can understand your point that it sucks even more if a story like this happens in a rich country. But I have to tell you that I personally can relate very well to the topic because hunger was wildly present in my childhood days. Of course, different from your mother, we had lots of company since almost everybody in our surroundings was poor.

I guess I should tell you about the stone cooking. Well! Get ready for a crazy story:

When I was a child the women of our family often didn't have enough food to give us as many meals as our greedy little tummies demanded. So they had to space the meals while trying to keep us content and in high hopes. Since everybody knew that the children would be utterly destroyed and unhappy if they knew that the next meal was still many hours away, they invented the comforting art of "stone cooking". First they sent us off to collect some firewood. We eagerly searched the surroundings for dry twigs and broken branches, all happy inside, since this meant that there would soon be some delicious food to share out. When we came back, we piled up a decent stack in front of the house, and a big cauldron was placed on top of it. The women filled the pot with water and secretly placed a few stones and herbs inside. To us the stones on the ground of the kettle looked like there were actually some vegetable bulbs and a good hunk of meat. So we got all excited with anticipation.

Next the fire was emblazed, and we were sent off for play. We ran around in a good mood, knowing that it couldn't be much longer until dinner was ready. You see, it was such a warm, comforting feeling to know that our kettle was full and our dear mothers and aunts already busy with the preparation of our next family meal. Every time some of us kids sneaked up to the women and expectantly asked how much longer it would take, the women just kept stirring the huge pot with great effort and smilingly sent us away again, indicating that our delicious stew would just take a little longer to get done. And so we played some more and got involved in our games to the point that we completely forgot about our hungry stomach for a long time. After all, a mouth-watering meal was almost ready and we would soon be called for dinner. Then we'd all sit down around the big pot and enjoy our food together. With lots of laughter, joking and happiness. And with this incomparable feeling of bliss that miraculously comes along with a full belly. That warm, strong feeling in the stomach that floods the whole body with a sensation of deep instant satisfaction.

And believe it or not, with this trick the women kept us happy until the next real meal could be served. It sounds crazy if you tell that story today, but those were the days of my childhood.

I haven't thought about the "stone-cooking" for a long time, but reading your last mail has suddenly triggered that memory. It's so strange how you never can know beforehand what might come up next from the hidden depths of our long neglected memories.

Hope you'll enjoy reading this story as much as I've enjoyed writing it down for you.

I wish you could be right here with me now, resting your head against my shoulder while I'm telling you sweet stories of long lost times that pop up in my mind like soap bubbles.

I love you, Linda.
Don't get mad at me. I am well aware that we don't know each other yet in real life. But what we share here is so real to me, and I just can't help feeling the way I do.

Sleep well, my love.
Sweet dreams.

Yours,
Stephen

9th of August
Oh Stephen!

I really appreciated your story. It sure is a bit crazy but in a charming way.
But say, wasn't this a tremendous waste of firewood?

It was also a bit surprising that you told me that you love me. I really hadn't expected that. I have to admit that I also start to develop feelings for you that confuse me a bit. I don't know if it is a good idea to give in to that growing affection. Maybe that way we'll both be unhappy in the end because of the distance between us. You know, if we should come to the point where we miss each other's physical presence too much, it might get complicated.

Love,
Linda

10th of August 2011
Dear Linda,

You are right. Loving each other might be complicated. But I believe there is a solution to every problem. We shouldn't limit our feelings. We should be thankful to have them.

Today, on my way home, we were surprised by sudden heavy rainfalls. Obviously the rainy season has started earlier this year than normal. When the locks of the skies suddenly and unexpectedly opened, everybody just headed for cover and I ended up with several other people in an open shelter with nothing but a canvas roof. Next to me there was this couple. They ignored everything around them and started kissing very passionately. I could hardly endure to watch them. It made me wish so much you were here too, and I could just keep you close to my pounding heart. Oh, Linda! That wish to hold you was almost unbearable. I have to admit that I start dreaming again. Do you think we will ever manage to meet each other in person? Would you consider it at all?

By the way, it was not a waste of firewood in those days to perform the "stone-cooking". Wood was one of few things we had plentiful.

Sleep well, my love. It's late. I had to stay in that shelter for almost four hours due to the rain, so I came home very late. My bike needs some repairs, so I'll have to get up early again in order to beat traffic.

Stephen

11th of August 2011
Dear Stephen,

Sounds like the rainy season is a romantic time in your country. ☺

Well, as to respond to your question, I would definitely consider meeting you in person. You know that I love travelling anyway. So, why not come to Accra?! Just thinking about it right now, I already feel a sensation of overwhelming excitement. Maybe we should really do that! Of course, there will be quite a few things to get organised before; fundraising, vaccinations, visa, someone to take care of my kids and so on. So, don't be afraid that I might show up in front of your door already tomorrow evening.☺

Thinking about it in a realistic way, according to my experience, if you want tickets for a good price, you need to book at least half a year in advance. So maybe I should start searching the internet for reasonable options.

What do you think about this? I guess I could probably manage to get away for a week in the beginning of February. We have a week of holidays then, which was originally introduced as a so-called energy- saving- holiday in mid-winter, and in the meantime has become a tradition. Christmas I have to spend with my family and for Easter I plan to go to Tenerife with my two youngest daughters.

I mean, it's now August, so it will still be almost half a year before February comes. But I think people need something to live up to. Something that keeps us going. Of course, with this long-term planning there is one serious question to be considered: Will we still be interested in seeing each other in half a year? Because in case we suddenly stopped contact at any time between now and February, I probably couldn`t undo the deal anymore. That means we should be absolutely sure about that.

I hope I'm not interrupting your innocent dreams with my plans to bring them down to earth. Maybe it is still too early to consider such realistic plans. Maybe you prefer to keep dreaming from a distance. Maybe we should leave things as they are, and enjoy what we have between us instead of risking that reality might kill our dream. I'm afraid, I don't know.

What do you think about all of this?
I'm looking forward to hearing your answer.

Yours,
Linda

12th of August 2011
Linda, my darling!

You just can't imagine how happy you have made me with your last letter. I feel so truly honoured and privileged to have a friend like you. Of course I would love to see you here in Accra at any time you choose. For me it's all the same. I'm always here, ready to have you as a guest at all times. It's definitely a big step in our relationship to meet in person. I don't know what to expect. I've got no experience along that line. But I am not afraid. I think we should just trust our feelings. And I guess it's normal to have a few doubts at times. That's just human, so we shouldn't feel bad about it. And look, even if anything should come between us, we can still meet as friends. I think we can always stay friends, no matter what.

There is no guarantee that we can be lovers. Not for now and not for the future. But I think we can promise to stay friends. Close, loyal friends forever! Do you agree?

So please, feel free to go ahead and find a good deal for a flight. Hope it won't be too expensive. I don't want you to go broke because of me.

Love you,
Stephen

13th of August 2011
Dear Stephen,

I can hardly believe I really did that but I have booked a flight to Accra which will arrive there on the first of February. Just think of it. We will really see each other in five months! So far it still doesn't sound real to me. But I guess five months is enough time to get used to the idea. You know, making such arrangements is all about creating future memories. Now, this moment in time that will be for us has been set in history. And the sequence of regular days that come and go without leaving too much impression on our mind will be like a river that causes us to drift closer to each other day by day until we finally meet in due season.

By the way, you are right about love and friendship. And I agree that it's impossible to vow love for life. But we can make that promise to stay close, loyal friends for all times.

Love,
Linda

14th of August 2011
Oh, my god, Linda!

You really did it?! I can hardly believe it! Hope that everything will go fine.

Thinking about it I'm totally flashed at the moment. Thrilled with the idea that now we share a dream that exclusively belongs only to the two of us.

I will start already now to make plans for your coming. Would you want to stay with me or rather choose for a hotel? Of course, I'd love to have you in my place, but as you know, I'm living here with my two children, and there is not really a lot of space in my modest, little house. Besides, you know about my relatives that live next-doors. They would certainly be very nosy, and we wouldn't have any privacy.

Is there anything in particular you would want to do here in Accra? Feel free to tell me which touristy sites might be interesting to you. Next time I'll attach a couple of tours and day trips from local travel agencies. But first I have to find time to go there.

Hear from you soon.
Yours always,
Stephen

15th of August 2011
Dear Stephen,

Don't worry about putting me up. I would anyway prefer to stay in a hotel. You can look
around for reasonable accommodation and maybe send me pictures and price lists. I'm sure we
will find something that comes in hand.

As for what I want to do there, I have to admit
that I don't have any idea what one can do in
Accra. I didn't even know that there are actually
tourists going there. Here in Europe most people
wouldn't consider going to such a country. Many
individuals hardly know that Ghana exists.

Looking forward to the announced materials on
local tourism.

Yours,

Linda

23rd of August 2011
Dear Stephen,

It's now been more than a week that I didn't hear
anything from you. I wonder what has happened.
Did I say anything that offended you? If I did, it
was not my intention. Was it maybe my remark
that I hadn't imagined Accra to be a place of
interest for tourists? I realise that my words

might have sounded a bit blunt, and I wish to apologise for them.

Hope to hear from you again soon.
Linda

30th of August 2011
Dear Stephen,

By now it's been two weeks that I've last heard from you, and it looks like you have stopped writing for good.
Wasn't it you who insisted on that promise that we would never leave each other without an explanation? And now you have left just like that. And I don't know why. The only thing that I could think of is that remark of mine concerning tourism in Ghana. Or maybe you have changed your mind about our personal meeting in Accra? I'm just writing one more time in case my mails might have got lost.
I am very sad that our promising friendship has ended so suddenly and unexpectedly.

Anyway – take care,
Linda

1st of September 2011
Linda, my love!

I am so utterly sorry that I have not been able to write to you in the past weeks. Please forgive me!
But due to the rainy season my internet connection was extremely instable in recent weeks. It has also been a real fight to get from A to B because of severe flooding. Today is the first day that at least the internet café is open, and I'm writing to you from there but will not be able to stay long since it's such a struggle to get home. To be honest it's not a nice place, and it bothers me to be surrounded by all those scammers. It makes me ashamed of being African. Really!!
Anyway, I will write to you again in detail as soon as possible. So please don't worry about anything.

Yours,
Stephen

2nd of September 2011
Oh, Stephen!

I was so happy to hear from you again! Now that I know the reason why you can't write, everything is fine. Don't worry. You don`t have to go to the internet café where you have to pay for every minute. I can wait until things are ok again, and then I'll be there as always.

Looking forward to things getting normal again in your place. Take care and make sure you are getting to work and home safely.

By the way, what's it with the scammers in the internet café?

Love,
Linda

7th of September 2011
Dear Linda,

Thank god, everything is under control again and my internet can be used as before.

This recent situation has really shaken me up. I was so afraid I might never be able to reach you again. Just imagine if all of a sudden the internet broke down for good and the only means of communication we had shared was the e-mail address from that website! Just think of it!

In my attachment I've sent you my private e-mail, my phone number and if all modern tech-nology should fail, also my snail mail addresses both from my home and from the hospital where I work. I've also given you the phone number of the hospital because in case of disaster this line will probably work better than the private individual lines. We just have to make sure that no such incident that is out of our control can get between us. It would be so horrible if we were separated, just because of something like this.

Well, since you've asked, the scammers in my country really are an issue. There are so many of them in the meantime. And I'm well aware that they are the reason why many people don't want to have friends or pals from Africa. When sitting in the internet café, I felt so ashamed of those people. And so furious at the same time. Believe it or not, about 8o to 90 percent of all people who use the internet café here are scammers. Some try to sell animals abroad. They show you sweet pictures of puppies and claim that those animals used to belong to their daughter or whosoever; and that this person unfortunately has died and they, on their part, are unable to keep them due to financial reasons. So they offer to give the puppies away for free, just to enable them to have a better life somewhere else. Now, as soon as people write back and show interest, they inform them that despite of the fact that the puppy is for free, there will be a few costs coming up. First there is money needed for required rabies shots and health certificates from the vet. And next, of course, the cash for the flight ticket. You would be amazed how many people actually send money. Of course, in the end the animal in question never arrives, and they cannot be reached anymore. They just change their online account and start the same fraud again in a different place. It's good business, but still I don't understand how a human being can have so little dignity. And of course, there are all those people who engage in the love-business. They open some internet account and join dating sites. Then they establish contact with individuals who preferably live in some wealthy country. Once they have won their trust, they start asking them for money. Always pointing out how utterly sorry they are for doing so and how much they love their new friend. Some are even so manipulative that they don't openly ask for cash. They just keep telling heart-breaking stories about their sick mother who urgently needs an operation or the unfortunate sister who has to care alone for several children and needs support and so on. And at some point people in rich countries seem to feel ashamed about their own privileged situation and have the urge to help. Better than giving money to organisations, they feel. Rather help a person they personally know and trust. And you wouldn't believe it, how much money people send! Incredible!

And, sad to say, I know that even my nephew is engaging in such scamming business. You know, the son of this brother I mentioned before. The one who is no good. Well, guess what he's been doing for the past years? He was too lazy for school and too much of a sluggard for regular, honest work. But he is quite an elusive character. He started writing to people in Europe and the USA, claiming that he and his friends were poor African students who were caught in the unfortunate situation of not being able to afford a laptop. He always points out how much these laptops would be essential for study-progress and how thankful he would be if people could send him their used laptops instead of throwing them away. And week by week people forward him laptops, at times used but next to new and sometimes even completely brand-new. Then he sends them sweet and appreciative thank-you-notes and with a bit of luck they might even send regular donations to help finance his studies. In the meantime my nephew has established a prosperous business selling all those donated computers, and he can live well on it. He is very vain and arrogant in his behaviour, and he thinks he is the only smart fellow around, showing open contempt and disrespect for anyone who holds an honest job. It makes me feel sick to my stomach that such a person is living right next to me. And it makes me feel ashamed that such a scammer is a close relative of mine.

But you know, money really has the say around here. Whoever manages to make money, no matter how, will be respected. It's sad but poor people often cannot afford morals. As for myself, I still keep my pride. No matter how poor and needy I could get some day, I would always prefer to work. It's a matter of dignity. I wouldn't be able to bear looking at my own face in the mirror if I made my money with foul tricks like this.

Oh, Linda! We shouldn't waste away our time, talking about scammers. But it's a serious issue, and people should be aware of it. Thank you for listening to this. It felt good to share my heart with you as always.

How is your family?
How is little Cora?

Hope to hear from you soon.

Love,
Stephen

8th of September 2011
Dear Stephen,

So happy to hear that your internet is functioning again. Thanks for trusting me with all your attached data.

The information about scammers was interesting to me. I have to admit that I don't have so much experience with internet friends on an international level. I hadn't realised so far that this seems to be such a commonly present issue.

Little Cora is fine and enjoying her life.
School has started again for Lori, and I think she is happy to see all her friends again and make music at school on a regular basis. Around here many families are from some other countries like Turkey, Serbia, or Poland and they use the nine weeks of summer vacation for a longer stay in the countries of their origin. Since we are always here in Vienna in summer, I guess it can get a bit boring for the children at times. But since my mother's death, we don't have relatives abroad anymore where I could send the children. And besides I don't want to go anywhere in summer when everything is flooded with tourists.
For Kate things changed a lot just a few days ago. Since she doesn't wish to continue with her schooling, she has now started an apprenticeship

in the restaurant of a large local furniture department store. She wants to become a cook and so far she is quite hyped with her new job. I'm not so sure about it because I know that this can be a tough life. But she is a physically strong and healthy girl, and besides she is quite practically-minded. So maybe she can manage. I originally had different plans in mind. The previous year I discovered a possibility here in Vienna that enables you to become a sports teacher without taking the rather demanding "Matura" exam which you normally need here for studying. So last year was dedicated to preparing for the entrance examinations which are quite tough. It soon turned out that Kate lived in illusions concerning her actual fitness standards. So there was a lot to work on. I even ordered a climbing rope from the internet so she could practise at home and I bought one of those heavy balls (I think they are called shots) for an athletic discipline called "shot-put". I got her registered in a better gymnastic club where she could train for all those categories required in the entrance exam, like uneven bars, parallel bars or balance beam. She also had a problem with running fast enough, so at times I even ran with her myself for practise or I went with her to a proper running lane and timed her. This wasn't exactly easy for me because due to a former injury my hip remained in a permanent state of instability. So, that makes it risky and almost impossible for me to do any sports. Finally I signed her into a specific preparation class, organised by the university. It was a full day course during our Easter vacation. I myself was on a holiday in Cuba at that time together with Clarissa. She had arranged a friend of hers to take care of the children during our absence. After a few days we were informed by that girl that Kate had been to this class only once. On that first day she just went there without having much breakfast and then it turned out that they had to do intensive and strenuous sports hour after hour with practically no chance to eat and drink in between. She told us later that some of the participants who obviously had already experience with the situation used the short breaks between lessons to quickly run to their lockers to stuff in some highly caloric chocolate bars and pour down some energy drinks. But since the official info materials didn't mention the need to bring sufficient food and drink along, Kate wasn't equipped properly. There was a lunchbreak, but it wasn't long enough to go home. And again, for buying a snack right there, she didn't have the necessary money with her. So the poor girl remained all day long without eating anything but an apple and nothing to drink but water from the tap. In the evening, when the classes finally ended, Kate walked home. She lost her way and strayed around in some unfamiliar neighbourhoods in growing despair. Somehow she finally managed to make it back home. And there, after resting a bit, she could suddenly not get up again. She tried to stand up but collapsed. The only person present was Lori, and she called that friend of Clarissa's who at that time was in a concert and therefore hard to reach. The poor young woman was a bit out of her depth. So she first called her mother, who is a medical doctor, and asked for advice. Then she arranged for the ambulance to come. Kate was taken to hospital where it turned out that there was actually nothing wrong with her organically. The whole problem was due to lack of food and fluid while training excessively. The doctor explained that during such an intensive training period the human body needs 5000 calories a day and five to six litres of isotonic liquid. Kate could soon go home again, but she still had to rest for a couple of days. By then the week was almost over, and it didn't make much sense anymore to go to that training class on the last two days. So, after that incident I had the feeling that this was maybe not really for Kate. She's good at sports but again not that good. Not like Clarissa who is an exceptional talent. So I just hinted to her that she didn't have to do it. That there were other options what to do in life. I think she was quite relieved to hear that. Next we had to opt for some "Plan B". After several trips to the Job

87

Agency, she chose for cooking, and luckily she still found a restaurant where she could start in September. Finding a place so shortly before the official start of our school-year can be quite complicated here. Actually most businesses select their new apprentices for September already in the previous February! Luckily it still worked out, and so far they are quite pleased with her performance. Even if the training last year was not enough for the sport university, at least it seems to be an advantage now because good physical condition and fitness are definitely a plus.

Hope your children are also fine.
Cora wags her little tail for Penny.

Sleep well,
Linda

9th of September 2011
Dear Linda,

I was shocked to hear about your daughter's unfortunate experience at that sport training. It's incredible how irresponsible those trainers have acted. They really should have informed in detail about this specific situation. Incredible that a girl of fifteen is asked to do sports until she has a physical breakdown! I mean, I sometimes see people here in the hospital where I work who break down because of overwork, and they have little choice because they are poor and have to take any work they can get.

Sometimes I am quite surprised about the things you tell me. It is also new to me that a girl in a civilised country is already working at the age of fifteen.

Anyway, best wishes for your daughter!

As for my children, I have to pay quite a bit now for my oldest son's secondary school. I have to pay school fees, and besides I need to finance a tutor since it seems he won't make it without additional support.

Penny wags back for you guys.

Love,
Stephen

10th of September 2011
Dear Stephen,

Today I got a shot for yellow fever which is required for entering Ghana. At least it lasts for ten years. At this institution where I went, they officially give you advice on which vaccination to get when travelling. But I have to say this advice turned out to be mostly advertising their shots and medicines. For example, they don't give you a prescription for the malaria medication I prefer. Obviously because they promote a different product. Normally I can get any serum from a friend, who is a doctor, but in the case of yellow fever you need an official stamp given by a certified institution. So I couldn't avoid going there. I have to say I'm proud of myself. They sure tried to talk me into getting more vaccinations but I managed to get in and out with nothing but the yellow fever shot.

In the meantime I found out that there is no embassy of Ghana here in Vienna. The closest one is in Switzerland. So I'm given the option to take a trip to Zurich or to send them my passport along with all other documents and money. And then I can expect to get the passport back within four weeks. I don't exactly like the idea of not having my passport for weeks. Besides it could get lost in the mail. Even if it is registered, I never trust them.

The good news: My daughter Clarissa is willing to stay in my place during this week when I go to Accra. So at least the kids should be taken care of properly. They really like Clarissa. She is very good with children and animals. Cora freaks out every time she sees her, jumping around in circles and cutting capers.

I've also looked at the brochures you've sent me. I think I'd prefer the local hotel in the centre of town. The other one is such a typical tourist set-up, and in this case I don't want that. Could you try to find out if they have rooms with bathtub?

Yours,
Linda

13th of September 2011
Dear Linda,

I practically feel guilty because you have to go through so much trouble in order to come here. Hope it all works out fine.

Seems there is really not much contact between Ghana and Austria if there is not even an embassy.

I think, I will tell you something about Accra and tourism today. It may well be that for many European countries Ghana is not a place of interest. But we do have tourists. Many of them are wealthy African-Americans who wish to return to their roots. You know, nowadays, with all the possibilities modern gene analyses offer, it is possible to do a gene test and find out exactly from which African country and even from which specific tribe an Afro-American person derives. So this has started an increasing interest in African countries and a great deal of tourist arrangements that specifically cater to those people. And you have to know: Very close to here is Cape Coast Castle which was originally built by the Swedish in 1653. In 1663 it was conquered by the Danish, and in 1664 the British took over. At first it was a Trade Centre, but later on it became the largest trans-shipment-centre for slaves in the entire world. Nowadays it's a World Heritage Site listed by the UNESCO.

Directly under the castle there is the slave dungeon. In this place without light up to 2000 people were chained together. They were naked and had no toilets. Food was thrown on the ground, like for animals. In such horrible surroundings they had to wait up to three months before they were finally branded and shipped. Many of them didn't survive this torture and died even before shipping. The last thing they saw before leaving was the DOOR OF NO RETURN. It had that name because past that point they would never see their home country again. If they survived the transport across the Atlantic, they were sold as slaves in the New World.

We will definitely go there when you are here. It's quite impressive! So, Cape Coast Castle is on our list for sure! Besides we will go to Kwame

Nkrumah Memorial Park. It's nice there during the day. Another place that I like very much is Kwame Nkrumah Circle. It's one of my favourite places here in Accra which offers a spectacular night view, and we can walk along to a nearby night market and enjoy a drink there. Since you love plants, I think we should also visit the Aburi Botanical Gardens.

I've already asked about the bath tub in the Grand View Hotel. They do have rooms with bathtub available.

Tonight I will still go to the Kwame Nkrumah Circle, and I know that I will mostly think about you while I'm doing some shopping nearby. Wish we could already now take a stroll there at night, hand in hand with all these beautiful coloured lights on. Even though you are not here yet, I can ensure you that I will take you to this favourite place of mine right in my heart. Wherever I go, you are always with me. Always on my mind and always in my heart. I love you, Linda! Now and forever.

Yours always,
Stephen

14th of September 2011
Dear Stephen,

Sounds like Kwame Nkrumah Circle is a great place to be and I don't mind at all accompanying you there tonight. Even if it is only in our phantasy. But: In only four and a half months I will actually be there! Just think of it!
And then we'll really take a walk there together. Isn't the prospect of this amazing?

It was interesting to hear about Ghana and the Slave Market, and of course I'll enjoy going there with you. Even though it sounds a bit depressing.
How do you feel about those times nowadays? Do you have personal resentment towards white people, deep down in your heart? If so, I could well understand.
Looking at history, it can give you the creeps. All these things which white people did to the black ones during slavery times. And in my place all these horrible things that Germans did to the Jews. And not to forget, all the crimes white conquerors did to the natives of the New World. And if we look at the world today, there are still so many wars. So much manslaughter and killing. In the name of some nation. In the name of some religion. Somewhere in the world, there are always people and governments that do awful

things to their enemies and sometimes even to their own people.
Why do people do that?
I really don't know.

I have to stop now.
Take care and sweet dreams.

Yours,
Linda

15th of September 2011
My dearest Linda,

I was thinking about your question a lot, trying to really search my heart. Do I feel personal resentment against white people because of the slavery times? What a question! Well, I know that many people have a very simple concept of dealing with this matter. About the bad white people who enslaved the poor black people. Of course, this was one of the most negative aspects of Africa's encounter with white man's civilisation. Apart from exploiting the riches of our continent, gold, diamonds, and minerals. But on the other hand the local African governments wouldn't have had the know-how to get a hold of all those resources that required mining and technology; so we couldn't have profited of them on our own, anyway. Besides, not everything the white people did was all bad. They brought us a lot of their advanced knowledge concerning medicine and established basic education, they taught us about their religion and eternal life in our saviour Jesus Christ, and even today they are still helping us to catch up with modern civilisation in so many ways. Even help us to control aids.

I'm going to say something now that might be surprising to you: I'm truly convinced that African men are evil. Very dark spirit. Black magic and voodoo. You know, only by the grace of Christ can African men be saved. And many don't even want to be saved. Rather keep practising primitive old rituals of witchcraft.

I've researched a bit about slavery on my own, and I'll share with you a few facts that almost nobody knows. You have to keep in mind that in the old days Africans were not a united people. There were many different tribes, and there were always some tribal wars going on. And it was general practice that the winners of those conflicts sold the members of those other tribes whom they had captured in the course of warfare to Arab traders. And those later sold them at the slave-market. So, sad to say, it was African people who sold other African people as slaves.

And even worse: Some people had children who were a bit rebellious in their teenage years; and if the grown-ups felt offended by their behaviour, it happened more often that they sold them to the Arab slave-traders. Often for no more than a sack of tobacco or a bottle of whisky. Just to get rid of them for good. Isn't that awful!? That's why I say: African man is evil. Of course, nobody talks about this bit of fact. It's so much easier to point your finger at the evil white slave-owners. So, actually I feel that slavery was at least in part the fault of black people too. At that time people were needed for work in the New World. And the American Indians were no good for work. I know that there was some priest who felt sorry for the local natives who all died in large numbers due to overwork. He found out that there existed slave-markets along the African coasts. And he had the idea that instead of collecting Indians, one could better legally buy Africans. They bought an already existing product from an already existing market and I can't even blame them for that.

Linda, my love, I have to sleep now.
Let me kiss you good-bye!

Stephen

15th of September 2011
Dear Stephen,

Oh my god! I really have to say that your last mail just blew my mind. How can you see it that way! I have quite a few African-American friends in the USA. They are usually very touchy when it comes to the topic of slavery. And I guess they would consider you a traitor.

I mean, I personally was well aware about the already existing slave-markets in Africa. Slavery hasn't been invented in America. It also has nothing to do with white people oppressing coloured individuals. At least not originally and not out of principle. One time I've even seen an old painting showing a rich African woman being served by her white slave!

Slavery was an old, wide-spread tradition. Just as you mentioned. Not only in Africa. Also during the Roman Empire or in the days of Alexander the Great, it was common to have slaves for rich people. And those people sold as slaves usually were prisoners of war. Their life wasn't always miserable in those days. The miserable part was having lost their freedom, of course. But on a day to day basis a lot depended upon the personal attitude of the people who had bought them. Greek slaves were usually valued because of their high educational standards, and rich Romans often used them to teach their children.

Others of course, tortured and abused their slaves. Even then religion had a clear point of view concerning this topic as specified in the bible. Masters should stay masters but treat their slaves in a fair way, and slaves should stay slaves and respect their masters. So: Unfortunately, Christian religion had no basic refusal of slavery. This of course came in hand when establishing slavery, centuries later in Christian America.

And even if it's true that slaves were legally bought and sold from an already existing market, the circumstances were so absolutely tragic and heart-breaking. And trading slaves became a very profitable business then, more than ever before in history. But I guess this was the law of the market. The known mutual reaction between supply and demand. And the growing markets overseas just needed more and more slaves. So it all got completely out of hand. And the way things developed, it was the beginning of a long-lasting dark chapter of American history.

You know, I really wonder if this opinion of yours that black people are evil and that they also had an active part in establishing slavery is truly your own opinion; or is it maybe an opinion some church has installed inside of you? Seems in Africa they tell you, African men are evil. In other places they tell them, *all* men are evil. And of course, women are evil. Basically the root of all evil since it was Eve who misled and seduced poor Adam. You know, I have a basic mistrust when it comes to churches and moral issues. Or when it comes to religions and social issues. Throughout history, churches always tended to be on the side of the rich. Always backing up the establishment. They are inclined to blame it all on you. If you are poor, well, you've just been too lazy to work your way up to riches. Of course, always ignoring the fact that most poor might well have to work for at least ten lives, considering their low pay, in order to get near anything that could be considered wealth. And if you make a mistake, it's because man is naturally evil and can't be good on his own. So, that way they have made it clear that you need the church since you are far too stupid to live a humane life without their guidance. This is how you create dependency. I'm so sick of hearing about it. This continuous introspection in search of our evil thoughts and deeds is no good. It's just depressing. Thinking about how bad we are, will never help us be any better. We have to connect with our quality, not with our shortcomings.

What was completely new to me was the bit of fact on people selling their own rebellious children for a bottle of whiskey or some tobacco. This is rather strong stuff! Hard to imagine, but of course, if you've researched on it, I believe you.

I hope I haven't offended you with my remarks about churches and religions. But I've had a lot of bad experiences along that line.

Let's call it a day, now!
Sleep well.
Yours,
Linda

16th of September 2011
Dear Linda,

I am sorry to hear that you had such bad experiences with regard to religion. To me personally religion is an important part of my life. Every Sunday I socialize with the fellow members of my church alongside with most of my other relatives; and I guess I would really miss it. I like singing and dancing in church even though I'm not much of a singer. And I highly appreciate this feeling of security and divine safety in Christ. You know, we are all in the hands of God, and he cares for us. No matter how hopeless and bleak things might seem at times, the Lord will always be with us. Even while we are walking in the darkest night the Lord is our light and our salvation. All the hardships of life are actually just trials; yet in the end the victory will be ours. The devil is very strong, you know. But we have to overcome the temptations of the devil's dark kingdom. Only the Lord can make us good!

I cannot imagine living without the comforting teachings of my church. Don't you feel lost and desperate at times? To me life would seem utterly hopeless and senseless without my faith. It's the promises of my religion that make life bearable and keep my spirits up. It's only the Lord.

What kind of bad experiences did you have with religion?

And don't worry about offending me along that line. It's not your fault if people in your church have failed you. Individuals make mistakes, and others suffer from them. As I've said before, man is evil and no good without the guidance of the Lord.

Besides, I still have to tell you something completely different tonight:

Little Penny is now old enough for breeding. I have already found someone who has a nice male. It will cost a lot, because here you have to pay for the male to get your female pregnant. But

I'll manage. In the end it will be a good invest-
ment once we can sell the puppies. The children
are already excited about having baby-dogs in
the house. I'm sure it will be a nice experience
for them.

Sleep well for now.
Yours,
Stephen

17th of September 2011
Dear Stephen,

Actually I'm quite familiar with all this churchy
talk. All these phrases and bible quotes. So, it's
not that you can tell me anything new along that
line. A long time ago I joined a small fundamen-
tal Christian church, something that in Europe is
considered a sect. In the beginning I was very
convinced and fascinated with their lifestyle.
And yes, it felt good to believe that there is a
God that cares about every single human being.
But as time went on, I started to be afflicted by
growing doubts. And doubts were not allowed.
Doubts were of the devil. One time, just thinking
about it in my own liberal and creative way, I
mentioned that one actually had to feel sorry for
the devil. You know, considering the fact that the

devil originally had been the brightest angel and closest to God, the devil definitely had to be very unhappy because now he was so far away from god. And the world couldn't be complete until someday the devil too would be saved by the grace of Christ and back in his original position. Voicing this thought was too much, of course. A couple of narrow-minded elders immediately isolated me from the rest of their sheep. In their opinion I was possessed by the devil and there-fore a danger to the community. They even prac-tised some exorcism on me. It was scary, and in the end I learned to keep my thoughts to myself.

At some point I left this sect. It was hard to do. Hard to take responsibility for my own life and for my future. I went through many hardships in life. And my Christian beliefs actually turned out to be of no help at all. I wish it had been different because of course I felt lost and desperate and would have expected comfort and direction to arise from my faith. But this was not the case. I found myself alone and totally left to my own devices. And since that religious context didn`t help me, I had to learn how to survive without it.

In the meantime many years have passed, and a lot has changed in my life. For a long time reli-gion was no theme of interest to me. But this might change again in the future. Right now, I just don't know anymore what to believe. I can-not imagine that any of those religions can have the so-called truth. A religion tends to be like a corsage for your thoughts. And that's not for me. I don't want my freedom of thought to be restricted.

It's not that I don't believe in anything at all. I guess my concept of God just has grown out of that churchy mould. I cannot imagine God to be an old man as pictured in the bible. I cannot imagine him to be a man at all. God has to be someone far beyond sexuality. No male. No female. Not a person at all. A power. The power behind the universe, or something even greater. Something we cannot even comprehend yet. I think all these religions have created God after their own image. And they have given him shape and characteristics that complement the philosophical concept of a certain time and society. Women were of little value in biblical times and therefore God had to be a man. And of course, he had to have a son to save the world. You know, Christian religion has been quite misogynistic.

I might sound bitter. But don't worry, I'm quite fine. Actually I want to change the subject now. This discourse about religion is already getting much too extended.

Let's talk about something more up-lifting!
So … Penny will be a mother soon? That's good news and I can imagine that your kids are already excited. Mine would be too but in our situ-

ation it would be far too complicated to have a bunch of chipper puppies in the house. So, I guess they have accepted the fact that little Cora will not get babies. Besides, I imagine it very hard to give them away.

The only thing my family has ever bred were hamsters. Even those we couldn't give away in spite of the fact that we had arrangements with a local pet shop. We just postponed their delivery week by week until they finally were too old for the pet shop. And with puppies I almost feel like one couldn't do that to little Cora. She is way too developed and her feelings are far too human. I think she would have to keep at least her favourite one. You have to know that she has a toy animal bunny who is now her favourite child. To her these soft toys are alive in the same way as they are alive for children. She found that bunny somewhere in the street and adopted it instantly. Ever since, it's been her definite favourite and you can clearly see how attached she is to it. Considering all of this, Cora might probably be very depressed to lose all of her puppies. It's already a drama when I want to wash her soft toys. As soon as I put them into the washing machine she acts concerned, and as soon as possible she collects them again. So, I honestly feel it's the better deal for her to have toy animals which she can keep for life than having real babies which she would have to lose soon.

But it will definitely be exciting to hear about Penny and her babies.

Hear from you again soon.
Linda

18th of September 2011
My dear Linda,

I don't know all the details about your negative experiences with religion and faith, but I am so sorry. Already the few things you have shared with me make me aware of the fact that there must be a lot of hidden grief and disappointment in the background of it all. Whenever you wish to talk about any of this, feel free to do so. But I will not ask you more right now because I understand that you probably don't feel comfortable with the topic.

If you don't mind, I will pray for you. I'll pray that God can heal your soul.

Today we have brought Penny to the place where the male dog lives. And guess what happened! She just ran back home again. Obviously she missed us too much. Well, on one hand that's really cute, but on the other hand we just have to get her to stay there as long as she is in heat. So, from what I've heard they have chained her now in order to make sure she has to stay. I feel kind of sorry for her, but it has to be. We also miss her and are looking forward to having her back. It's so quiet in the house without her. Something is definitely missing.

In the meantime the rain has started again, and the rainy season is expected to last until the end of October. So in case you should suddenly not hear from me, our internet is most probably out of order again.

Your friend always,
Stephen

19th of September 2011
Dear Stephen,

Thanks for your kind and understanding words concerning the religious issue.
And I don't mind if you want to pray for me.

Hearing about Penny, I felt so sorry for her. What a sweet character. What a little darling, running back home to her people immediately!

Hope you won't have too many problems with the weather.

Sorry, but I can't write much tonight. I have a new student for English lessons, and what he does in school is quite complicated, so I still have to take the time to get some materials together for him.

I'll write more next time.

Take care,
Linda

26th of September 2011
Dear Stephen,

After not having heard from you for a full week, I have to admit that I have really missed exchanging my thoughts with you.
Thank you so much for your short phone call today. It was sweet to hear that you are still thinking of me. And I really like your voice.

Here in Austria summer is over by now and we have fall coming up. The trees have already started to change their leaves, and the foliage looks very pretty. All yellow, orange, shades of red and gold. This time of the year is called the Indian Summer, maybe you have heard about it. I'll send you some pictures of the trees in the park, so you can also see what I'm marvelling at with so much admiration.

Hugs,
Linda

15th of October 2011
My beloved Linda,

Finally things have improved here enough that I can write again.
Thanks for the beautiful pictures in the attachment. I really loved the one where little Cora is chasing happily through the colourful foliage. My god, she practically disappears in all those leaves, but she seems to have a lot of fun! And my favourite is of course, the one where you are leaning against that tree. Great picture! You definitely are a very beautiful lady, Linda. I really have to say that. Beautiful eyes and golden hair and such a sweet, reluctant smile. I'd just love to hug you right now and give you a little kiss on the forehead.
I've seen pictures of the Indian Summer in books but of course, never in person. I am glad to imag-

ine you in such a wonderful environment. We have here some trees that also get very red and impressive but with red blossoms.

My best piece of news I've saved for the end:
Penny returned already two weeks ago, and she definitely seems to be pregnant. According to my figuring, her offspring should be due by the end of November. So, I'll keep you informed. Right now the expectant doggy-mother has a very good appetite. She really wants to eat all the time. Besides, she cuddles a lot with my son on the couch. The two of them are very cute to watch.
So, let me give you one more kiss ...
Stephen

16th of October 2011
Dear Stephen,

Glad, you liked the pictures of the Indian Summer!
And congratulations to the expectant doggy-mother!
In my place everything is fine. Apart from the fact that Kate shows some growing aggressiveness since she has started working.
I mean, it's normal that kids fight. And they tend to get more abrasive during puberty probably due

to a rising hormone level. But there have to be limits. Sometimes it seems to get out of hand. And there are situations when I feel it's my responsibility to do something about it. But what? I feel so helpless most of the time. And I'm really afraid that if they cannot handle their aggressive fits, at some point something could occur that cannot be undone anymore. Sometimes I have such a feeling of severe danger, a fear that something horrible might happen.

You know, of course I'm aware of the fact that working in that kitchen is tough. Working class standards amongst people who are not exactly the winners of our society. Kate still claims that she likes working there, but my enthusiasm is limited. It's essential to her that people at the job think highly of her. But at the same time, me, Lori and even Cora have lost significance. She's also told me already that she will not walk Cora anymore. You know, I can understand that she feels too exhausted to walk her after a long day at work, but what bothered me most, was the way she communicated it. Just screamed in my face that this dog had been bought as a surprise for Lori and that she therefore had nothing whatsoever to do with it. This reminded me of the summer when we bought Cora while Lori was in the camp. I told you about it. We bought the puppy because Kate wanted it. She chose for it. She named it. And I had made it clear from the beginning that having a dog was meant to be a family project. And there was nothing left for Lori, apart from declaring the dog a "surprise". As I told you before, Lori was mourning her hamster and definitely not ready to love a new animal at that time.

Yet, even then, I had a talk with Clarissa where she mentioned how bad poor Kate felt about the fact that I "had bought a dog for Lori" … I really felt like an idiot at that point. Just imagine my situation! I, a person who doesn't even like dogs, was willing to accept a dog in our house for the sake of my children. Because they wished for one and because I felt it could be valuable for them to share a common responsibility. You know, I wasn't sure at that time if Kate had maybe misunderstood the situation, so I talked to her about it. Pointed out that this was a family dog and that she had had the biggest part in getting it, since I had actually intended a much longer phase of just visiting puppies and studying up on different races, and , of course, Lori was supposed to be part of that process. The decision for a specific puppy was definitely meant to be made by the three of us together. Guess what! When I talked to her about it then, she denied having said those things to Clarissa, claiming that Clarissa had probably misunderstood something. In our talk back then, Kate obviously knew quite well what the facts were. You know, I really tried to sort out any potential misunderstandings and she just answered that it was all clear to her anyway!

But now, after all that time, she has returned to that point of view, probably because it is a practical excuse for not walking Cora anymore. And in a certain moment it finally dawned on me that it probably had not been just a misunderstanding when she had told Clarissa about how sad she was that I had bought a dog only for Lori. Going by how protective Clarissa sounded when she told me about it, Kate must have done an excellent job at presenting herself as a poor, unfortunate girl whose mother only cares about her little sister …

Well, I can understand that she sometimes feels disadvantaged. And her behaviour seems to be quite successful because she gets lots of attention from her siblings that way. But you know, it upsets me a lot. It hurts me to see how she doesn't care about us and how other people fall for her exaggerated stories.

Oh my god, Stephen, this wasn't intended to get such a long and detailed report on domestic issues! I can hardly believe that I started it with the sentence, "Everything is fine apart from the fact …"

Next time I'll write about something more inspiring, I promise. Right now I feel kind of exhausted. These domestic problems really have a tendency to drag us down.

Well, I hope you don't mind reading all of this. It must have really burdened me a lot, because the moment I started mentioning it, the words just poured out and kept flowing.
How is the dream house?
How is Penny?
Love,
Linda

17th of October 2011
My darling little Linda,

Don't feel bad about telling me about your "domestic problems". These circumstances in our household do influence our wellbeing a lot and unfortunately they are not always under our control.
In this age of puberty children often get more aggressive than before. To me it seems that the rising level of certain hormones might have something to do with it. And I can understand that it is hard for you to deal with it, especially as a single parent. Yet I think that one shouldn't tolerate a lack of respect. You do so much for those children. You work so much to finance

them, so they should at least be thankful and re-spectful. Linda, please don't let those things get so close to your heart. I am there for you, and I want to hold you and support you. Don't forget, I will always be on your side!

The dream house?
Well, good news, I'm in the business of choosing some tiles for the roof, which I plan to order as soon as I'll have the money for Penny's puppies. What colour do you think looks best for the roof? I can choose between a large variety of colours and shades. I'll send you the catalogue with the samples. Right now I tend to prefer green, red, blue or purple. But I haven't found my favourite yet. What do you think? As you know, I always value your opinion.

Penny enjoys the sofa. She seems to need a lot of rest and has stopped playing with her toys com-pletely.

Take care, my love!

Yours,
Stephen

18th of October 2011
Dear Stephen,

Thanks for being so understanding. It is wonderful to have a friend like you.
Hmm ... talking about the roof of your house – Here in Austria a tiled roof tends to be red. That's the classical, natural colour of those tiles. I find it very interesting that you can choose from so many different colours but of course, if you glaze the tiles, you can have any colour you want. I still have to get used to the idea and so far I'm not so sure what to think about a house with a purple roof. So, instantly I would choose for red because it contrasts best with nature. The sky already offers a lot of blue and so does the water. Plants and grass are green. Red, on the other hand, seems to be the colour of manmade objects. I guess I just like white little houses with red roofs. Maybe, because they tend to look like that in Spain too, and I've always liked traditional Spanish architecture. But that's probably just what I'm used to. Probably, in a different country, houses and roofs in all kinds of diverse colours also look charming in their own way.
So, I'm afraid I can't be of much help right now. But I'm so happy your house is progressing!

Take care!
Linda

21st of October 2011
Dear Linda,

I'm sitting in the internet café again because right now I do not have electricity at home. You know, here in Accra you buy electricity with a prepaid card just like the ones you use for the phone and right now I can't afford a new card. It's no problem. I can do without it for a while. But it means that it will take some time until I can write again.

I don't want to stay here much longer, as you know, I dislike the atmosphere.

Just a quick kiss and a big hug from your friend Stephen.

22nd of October
Dear Stephen,

Don't worry. Everything has time. I hope that you can get everything arranged as soon as possible. Until then, a big hug from my side too.

Yours always,
Linda

22nd of November
Dear Linda,

Finally, after a full month, I'm able to write again. At least we have electricity now and a functioning internet. Unfortunately there are some problems again with my bike, so for the time being I have to get up very early again in order to make it to the place I work. But I don't wish to complain. Things are the way they are. And there is a lot to be thankful for.
How are you, my love?
What's new in your place?
Can't wait to hear from you,
Stephen

23rd of November 2011
Dear Stephen,

How wonderful that you are back! I really missed you.
In my place there is nothing new. In the end of October I had to spend quite a bit of time in the garden, just to prepare it for the winter season. It's a lot of work moving the pool upstairs to my room. It needs to be cleaned and ready for the fish because they have to spend the winter months indoors. Last year, I waited a bit too long

and suddenly there came some unexpected early snow. I still remember how icy my hands felt when I tried to get the goldfish out of that freezing water.

This year everything was settled in time. At the windows upstairs there are still some strawberries enjoying the cold sun of November, and since they face the south side, they actually still ripen which is very unusual around here.

Kate is busy at work, Lori is occupied at school, and I have a full schedule with my clients just as always.

How is Penny doing?

Love,
Linda

24th of November 2011
My sweet Linda,

I'm glad to hear that everything is fine in your place. Sounds romantic to have strawberries right at your window.

Thanks for asking about Penny. Well, according to my figuring those babies of hers should be due any day. Her belly is already quite round and she doesn't want to move much anymore. But so far there are no signs of labour. By the way, do you know exactly how long pregnancy takes in a dog? And is there a difference between large and small races? Because I'm not sure. Some people here say gestation time is eight weeks, others again say ten weeks is totally normal. With Penny it was in the end of August that she conceived, I guess, but I'm not sure if those eight weeks are counted from the day when she started to be in heat or from conception. Altogether it looks like labour could start at any moment. I've already arranged a mattress on the floor for her and the puppies because up on the sofa it's too dangerous for the babies. But so far Madam Penny is residing on the couch, as always. Hope we can convince her to stay down there as soon as the little ones are born. The children are already extremely excited and ask several times a day how long it will still take. But it's a nice kind of excitement. Kind of like waiting for Christmas.

Well, I really need to sleep now.
Let me hug you for a moment.

Love,
Stephen

25th of November 2011
Dear Stephen,

Unfortunately I am no expert when it comes to animal pregnancies. Therefore I really can't tell you how exactly this should be figured. But I´ve also read that gestation time in dogs is about eight weeks, so you can be prepared for action at any time.

The only animal babies we ever had were hamsters, a long time ago. We had bought them in Spain at the market. I mean, the first hamster we ever had was Mousy. At that time I didn't even know, what a hamster looked like. I was strolling along the market area in our Spanish hometown when my daughter Clarissa, who was then about four or five, pointed to some cage and told me that she wanted such an animal. I stopped and took a look. Then I asked one of the ladies, who were also watching, if these were mice, and she responded, "Yes, yes, cute little mice!" So, the next week we bought such a "mouse" and during the rest of our stay we often took it along in its handy little cage. People looked at it and more often someone exclaimed, "Look at that sweet little hamster!" And then I always explained that this was no hamster but a mouse. And guess what?! All these people, who actually knew damned well that this was a hamster, got quickly convinced that it was a mouse. And nobody dared to speak up against me. When we were back in Austria, I bought myself a book on how to handle mice. And somehow nothing matched. My mouse just behaved totally different. For example, it said in the book that you can keep mice on a table because they will never try to jump down higher than sixty centimetres. But my "mouse" jumped down from the table with a rather reckless attitude. It was during my next visit to the pet shop when I noticed a box somewhere in the background. Inside, partly hidden between a crisscross of hay, I could see some animals that looked a lot like my "mouse". So I asked the man if I could take a closer look, and he readily fished out one of the animals for me. No doubt! This creature looked exactly like my "mouse". So I asked him what kind of animals these were, and he said they were hamsters!! What really amazed me was that none of those people, who definitely knew more about biology than I, had been able to convince *me* that my mouse was a hamster. No, I got *them* to believe that this hamster was a mouse. Even though they knew better!! I thought a lot about this incident at that time and finally came to understand that if you just tell something wrong with enough conviction, people will believe it. Even if they actually know it's wrong. After all, we live in a time where everything is possible. Why not a mouse that looks like a hamster. ☺

What shocked me about it was how easily you can get people to question their knowledge. How quickly you can get them to mistrust their senses.

So you see I'm not really an expert when it comes to animals. The reason is that as a kid I was never allowed to have pets, due to the fact that my grandmother hated them.

Anyway, eventually we got a second hamster and at some point they had babies. And believe it or not Mousy gave birth in a hamster-ball. I don't know if you have ever seen something like that. At that time we saw a film on TV where a hamster was moving around the house in a ball made of clear, limpid plastic. That way it couldn't get lost, and at the same time it was protected from other animals while riding around in the whole flat. We found it kind of neat and investigated where one could buy something like that. Our hamsters loved the running ball dearly. And because they loved it so much, Mousy even gave birth in that ball!! That sure was a surprise when I wanted to put her back to the cage that day shortly before midnight. I didn't really know what to do. When Mousy saw me she started packing the little ones into her hamster-cheeks, and I was afraid she would eat them. You know, I had read in some book that they tend to eat them if they have stress. Well, anyway, I finally filled the whole contents of the ball back into the cage and hoped for the best. Mousy hadn't prepared a nest for her offspring beforehand, so she was very busy that night, tackling her new responsibilities. Everything was fine in the end. They were five babies and all of them females to our surprise. One of them missed a foot in the back, don't know if Mousy bit it off or if it was just a genetic defect. One of them died at the age of only a few months; maybe it fell down from somewhere, you know, with small children that can happen easily. Another one developed some digestive problems and suffered from diarrhoea all of its life but this was no big problem. Even though we had arrangements with a pet shop, we never brought them there in the end. Always kept them one week longer and in the end for good. I've already mentioned that before, haven't I? Well, I guess the handicapped and the sick one we would have had to keep anyway. They shared a cage all life long, even though hamsters normally need their own residence once they are grown-up. Since they were not in full health they probably lacked energy for more serious fights, but even those two quarrelled and ripped apart each other's ears. I mean, their ears are thin as paper! The others, though, were both big and strong and they hated each other so much that they couldn't even live in a cage with a dividing grate. They just kept snapping each other through the bars. Well, we finally put a wooden wall between them which solved the problem. But I have to say, those babies were never as cute as their parents. They just somehow lacked personality and charm. Maybe because we couldn't spend so much time with them. Hamsters only get tame if they interact a lot with humans.

Strangely enough they all died within one week when their lifespan was over. The sick one just as well as the two huge and healthy ones. As if their battery was just empty at exactly that time.

Not so long ago, when we had that hamster that died just before we got Cora, I tried to get him such a hamster-ball at the pet shop. And the owner told me that those balls were in the meantime forbidden because some animal-rights-activists were of the opinion that they presented cruelty to animals. Well, I told him then about *our* hamsters, and about how much they had loved running around in such a ball. As you can imagine he was quite surprised. It's always amazing to me how the appropriate way to keep your animal or to raise your kid or what to eat changes every couple of years. And what is "in" and "out" is just the fashion of a certain time or year.

Well, Stephen, I hope you enjoyed my hamster story while waiting for your darling puppies!

Take care, Linda

27th of November 2011
Dear Linda,

What a story! There is really something to that point that people will believe practically every-thing and anything if the so-called facts are just communicated in a convincing way. Just radiat-ing sufficient self-confidence might already do the trick because people are highly submissive, be it by nature or by education. And you are right: If it is that easy to get people to mistrust their own knowledge, even of facts they actually know, how easy will it be to convince them con-cerning other issues where they lack profound knowledge to rely on? It feels a bit spooky just to think about it. That it is really so easy to change other people's mind!

I enjoyed hearing about the hamsters. I didn't know so far that they could develop personality at all. How were the parents different from the children? What distinctions could you actually spot?
The hamster-ball sounds like great fun. Too bad they don't sell it anymore. But you know, if you look in some third world countries, you might run into a bunch of hamster-balls. That's how they always do it. As soon as something is for-bidden or out of fashion in developed countries, they transport the residual items to some Third

World Countries and try to sell them there. For example, when you come nowadays to Accra you can buy those walkers for babies even at the market. You know what I mean? It's a device with wheels and a solid metal frame with a fabric seat for the baby to sit in. Then, when the baby wiggles, this vehicle starts to move, and with a bit of practice the baby can run all over the room at quite some speed. Babies love walkers because of the mobility they gain. But I've heard from a Swedish volunteer, who used to work at our hospital, that in Europe walkers are considered dangerous in the meantime, due to some accidents that happened in the past. What do you think about that?

Penny still keeps us all waiting and the suspense is killing us by now.

Take care, my love.
Stephen

28th of November 2011
Dear Stephen,

I often think of you and Penny. It can't be long anymore …

As to answer your questions: Yes, hamsters can develop personality. Mousy was a very smart and charming creature. She was the only hamster I ever knew who actually liked to eat while lying in a human's hand. Normally they just take the food and stuff it inside their cheeks. But Mousy actually lay down on her back in a human's palm, stretched her hind legs comfortably apart and eagerly ate bit by bit holding the food with her tiny little pink hands. One time she got lost in the flat. We looked for her everywhere but couldn't find her. After some hours the search got to the point where we started moving heavy furniture. Then, all of a sudden, I entered the kitchen and saw Mousy sitting right next to my husband watching him, as he was pulling the fridge to the front. And she just sat there looking up to him!!

The male hamster was also very special. He was extremely small with white, long fur and black eyes. We named him "Little Bear" and the children just loved him a lot. In those days there was always someone at home and Little Bear was going from hand to hand. I guess he just got used to spending his life on children's hands to the point that he actually couldn't do without such close connection. We had him only for one year. When we were in Spain for the whole summer, he and Mousy died. I think they missed us too much. Just food and water isn't enough if you are used to love and attention all around the clock. Such an animal doesn't know that the children will come back again. For a hamster with a lifespan of only two years, a couple of months is a long time. Feels probably like a decade. Too long to keep up hope. They might wait for some days, but at a certain point they give up. And if this intensive communication with humans is the centre of their life, there remains nothing to live for anymore. And so they slip away and quietly retreat from their body till they die. Believe it or not, that day when Little Bear died, we were sitting in Spain in a restaurant next to the beach. And all of a sudden I could see Little Bear running across the table. And in the evening my husband told me on the phone that he had died.

The hamster we had before Cora was also a sweet one. His name was Crumble, but I often called him "Mr. Avocado". He just loved to eat avocado even though this is no recommended food for rodents. Good for him that I didn't find out about that until he was already a year old. I figured if it hadn't harmed him so far, it was probably ok for him to eat it. I just couldn't have taken it away from him by then. He would have missed it too much. He was one time sick with a big abscess on his little bottom which can be life threatening for such a small animal. But since he was tame enough, we managed to bath his bottom in camomile tea and gave him antibiotics and he completely recovered. By the time the abscess was ripe he just bit it open and then it quickly healed.

Talking about Mousy's and Little Bear's off-spring, I just couldn't tell you anything special or outstanding about them. I mean in the beginning, when the one who missed a leg started biting her sister in the ear, it looked like she had punched her a hole for placing an earring. Soon after that there was a cut. At some point there were two cuts that made this ear look like a shamrock. She was even named shamrock then because of that ear. But at some point there were also parts of the shamrock ear missing, and altogether even this story has nothing to do with great individual personality. The children never loved those wild creatures the way they were attached to Mousy and Little Bear.

As to respond to your other question: Yes, I do remember walkers. My children all loved them. And yes, in the meantime they are out of fashion because they are supposed to be dangerous. On one hand because they can tip over. Well, of course they can. Some people put a baby in a walker outside where the ground is uneven and let it race around there. And then they are sur-prised if the walker topples. I mean, that's something for a flat with an even floor. And besides you definitely have to supervise your baby. The other argument given against walkers is that the baby's spine is stressed too much by being forced into an upright position before it has the strength to support itself. Well, I don't know what to think about this. I remember times when older people cursed me because I was carrying my baby in a sling. They seriously believed that the baby would get hunched or the legs could get bent. Guess that were tales from times when babies didn't have enough vitamin D around here and therefore had very soft, bendable limbs. In those times children were wrapped tightly into their pillow and some people even bandaged their legs. Yet, children in other countries have been transported in slings all day for thousands of years, so obviously it wasn't the fault of the sling. Of course, in different places there are diverse factors that all add up to a certain condition. What functions in one place might fail to do so in another. It's like we said before: There are fashions for the use of such things and they seem to change faster all the time.

Best wishes for all of you.

Love,
Linda

29th of November 2011
Dear Linda,

Looks like Penny's babies will finally be born tonight. She's been already quite restless throughout the day and has stopped eating completely, which is unusual for her. Throughout the day I've massaged her lower back and her belly a bit because she seems to have pain. I've also arranged things as comfortable as possible for her on the couch since she still refuses to stay down on the floor. Well, with a big plastic table cloth to protect the couch and a big soft blanket on top, I think it should be fine. Hope it doesn't take too long …
I have to stop writing now, but I'll still come back to you later that night.

Love,
Stephen

29th of November
Dear Linda,

Finally after quite a few hours of labour the puppies have been born. Sad to say, one of them didn't make it. I guess he was just stuck too long in the birth passage. The others are alive but they still seem to have trouble nursing. So far they haven't drunk any milk from Penny, and I know that it is important that they drink the so-called "beast-milk" as soon as possible. I think it's also named colostrum and very essential for the immature immune system of both human and animal babies. Hopefully they can drink soon. Maybe they just need to rest a bit before doing so. Penny is being a good mother and has licked the three of them excessively right after birth and right now they are cuddling there together. I've put a bunch of mattresses, pillows and rags next to the sofa to protect the little ones from falling since Penny doesn't agree on leaving the sofa. The kids have watched the entire birth, and they have cried a bit because of the dead puppy. But anyway, there are still three live ones, so we can be happy, I guess.

I have to go back to them now. Just wanted to let you know the news. You are the first person I've told, by the way!

Love,
Stephen

30th of November 2011
Dear Stephen,

Congratulations to the doggy-mother. I'm sure she is very proud of her little ones. Sorry to hear about the one who didn't make it. Hope the three survivors are enjoying Penny's milk in the meantime so that they can get big and strong. Can't wait to hear more about them. Would be great to see a picture of them soon.
Cora and I send lots of love to all of you!
Yours,
Linda

1st of December 2011
Dear Linda,

Thanks for your congratulations. I have attached a picture of the doggy-family. They have drunk some milk in the meantime, but I think they should drink a lot more. They are quite small and still a bit weak, it seems. But so cute! I plan to keep the brown one with the white stripe and to sell the two black and white ones. Actually I have already people waiting to buy them. I hope they will turn out a nice mix. But Penny is very cute and the father is also a handsome dog, so they should come out fine. So far you can't say how they will look when they are older. Dogs of mixed race are always a surprise egg. You can never be sure.

Take care, Linda
Stephen

2nd of December 2011
Dear Stephen,

Thanks for the picture! Oh my god! They are so cute! Is the brown one a boy? He kind of looks like a boy to me. Penny sure is an excellent mother. I love it how she is lying there in this truly relaxed way with the little ones by her side. And this proud and direct look into the camera! By the way, why do you want to keep the brown one?
Wish to hear from you soon.
Linda

3rd of December
Dear Linda,

You are right, the brown one is a boy. The children have already fallen in love with him from the start. He snuggled up in David's hand shortly after birth. And then he made such a wee little sound – how can one not fall for such a creature. At first I thought that I couldn't fulfil my children's wish to keep him. But in the meantime I've changed my mind. Since he is a male, I want to keep him, so I can rent him out for breeding once he is grown-up. This might be an even easier way of earning some extra money than covering the costs of renting a male and going through all the trouble of pregnancy with your female dog. Well, of course, that's plans for the future! First our little ones need to grow a bit. But as we both know, time goes by so fast. I guess in a few weeks they will be eagerly roaming around the place. I just hope they won't make too much trouble … But if they do, it might make it a bit easier to see them leave when the time comes. I'm sure the children will miss them.

Take good care of yourself, Linda!

Yours,
Stephen

4th of December 2011
Dear Stephen,

Today my passport with the visa inside has returned from Switzerland, which is good news. And yes, in less than two months I will be with you in Accra. Just think of it! In the meantime the puppies will keep you occupied. I have to work a lot myself, which is normal for this time of the year. Sometimes I miss our long, extended mails, talking about all kinds of philosophical topics, but I guess we both don't have time to write so much at the moment.
So let me just give you a big hug for now.
Yours,
Linda

5th of December 2011
My dearest Linda,

Seems we both have a lot to do right now. Don't feel bad about it. I was so happy to hear that you are already all set to come here, to Ghana.
Nothing can stop us now from meeting in less than two months!!! Finally this event is coming close and starting to sound real!

Well, hearing from you was the only good news today.

Here in my house we are all a bit burdened because the little dogs don't seem to be fine. They were drinking normally lately, but now it seems that they are very weak again, and to be honest I'm afraid they haven't really grown much so far. This afternoon I discovered that one of the black and white females was in a very dehydrated condition even though Penny has milk. But maybe she hasn't enough, who knows. I still tried to feed her with a syringe but she was already too weak to drink anything at all. Soon after that she died right in my hand. It was hard for me to tell the children when they came home from school and happily stormed towards Penny's bed. They were so shocked that now another one is gone. I feel kind of empty and gone inside. Just sad. I mean, it's just a puppy, and you have to be prepared for something like that to happen. That's called natural selection, I guess. The survival of the fittest. And after all, a dog doesn't have such a high value here. So actually this feeling of grief I experience right now has totally taken me by surprise. I can't write more at the moment. Hope you can understand.

Love,
Stephen

6th of December 2011
Oh Stephen!

I'm so sorry to hear that. Just don't know what to say. And don't be surprised about your emotions. Feelings are feelings and if you love something it will always hurt to lose it. That's the price of love. Right now I'd just like to hug you and be with you to share your grief. How are the two remaining dogs doing?

Love,
Linda

7th of December 2011

Well, the other female has also not survived the night. When I looked after the dogs in the morning, I noticed that she didn't move anymore. Penny still nudged her and licked her frantically, doing her best to get her going again, but she was already dead. You can imagine! The children saw it in the morning as they were getting ready for school. I allowed them to stay home today because they cried so much. They wouldn't have been able to pay any attention in class anyway. I just hope that at least the brown one survives. He is everybody's favourite and luckily a bit bigger

than the others. So I guess he has better chances. Penny is taking good care of him and now that he's the only one, there should be definitely enough milk for him. At this very moment I see him nursing, and I can practically hear him smacking. So that's good news!!
Hear from you soon.

Yours,
Stephen

8th of December 2011

Oh no!! That's too bad!! I really feel for your children. It must be hard for them. I remember when our hamster Crumble died. Lori was just so heartbroken. And poor Penny, how does she take it?
I'm glad to hear that at least the brown one is fine and I keep my fingers crossed.

Love,
Linda

9th of December 2011
Dear Linda,

Thanks for your good wishes. I hope that at least the brown one will be here to celebrate Christmas with us. You know, I haven't told the children yet that I plan to keep him. It was supposed to be a Christmas surprise for them. So this one just has to make it!!
I do a lot of extra jobs at the private hospital right now. This is very necessary because I had already planned on the money that I would have made on selling the puppies. Now I've actually lost money with this dog breeding business because I've invested money for the male, about 350 euros, to be exact. Besides, I had extra costs for Penny's nutrition since she was really eating a lot during pregnancy, and I also bought her good quality food and vitamins to make sure she had everything she needed. So right now I have debts, but there is no need to worry. With the extra jobs I will be able to make up for it soon. Just Christmas will have to be modest this year, that's for sure. And the dream house will have to wait a bit until I can continue to invest in bricks and tiles again.
How do you celebrate Christmas?
Looking forward to hearing from you.
Yours,
Stephen

10th of December 2011
Dear Stephen,

I have a lot of respect and admiration for the way you manage your life. How you always make new plans and find alternative ways to improve your family's living conditions despite many obstacles. It's truly amazing that you can even bring alive a project like the dream house! And it doesn't matter if you have to postpone it a bit. It all has time.

I hope Christmas will be fine for your family and the brown puppy will comfort everybody's heart. It will surely be a wonderful surprise for the children if they actually get to keep him. Especially since he was anyway their favourite from the beginning.

Christmas in my family isn't all that special. As you know, I'm not religious, so there is actually nothing to celebrate. Personally, I've always hated Christmas since my childhood. You know, when I was little, my uncle always came to celebrate Christmas with us. I loved it a lot then. When I was about nine my uncle informed us that from then on he preferred to celebrate with his wife and son alone. I remember how much I cried. My mother told me to phone my uncle. Maybe that would change his mind, she said. But no, my uncle's mind was already set. His wife and his mother didn't get along. So his wife finally refused celebrating Christmas with my uncle's family of origin. And my tears were of no interest …

But even before, I remember, there were always those outbursts of fights and those ridiculous sensitivities about each and every word somebody had said. I guess it was always complicated for everyone.

When I was grown-up I didn't celebrate Christmas for quite a few years but as soon as you have children yourself, it's hard to get around it. It's such a big deal here! And of course, I didn't want my children to miss out. So all year long I collected offers from toy stores and hid them carefully. Guess I just took pride in the idea of giving every child a huge pile of presents, despite our forever strained money situation. You have to consider: Other children have families. If two sets of grandparents and a couple of aunts and uncles all give one present each, it quickly adds up to a considerable number of gifts. Unfortunately my children didn't have so many relatives who would care enough to make them presents. Besides there were four of them in those days when the older ones were little! Anyway, I just bought each of them ten presents myself. Bought them, wrapped them in gift paper and later on helped them to unpack them again. While I was doing all the work involved in preparing a reasonable Christmas Eve, my husband usually retreated to his room and closed the door. He just came out to serve himself the biggest part of the dinner I had cooked. Then he would go back to his room and listen to some opera music. He never had any interest in celebrating with us. In later years Christmas used to be one of the few occasions when all the family united, until two years ago the distressing situation between me and my oldest daughter escalated.

So now the family has broken up into different blocks that celebrate together.

I have to confess I'm always happy when Christmas holidays are over.

Love,
Linda

11th of December 2011
Dear Linda,

I can imagine that your family situation must be very burdening, but I have to admit that we have a similar problem here too, due to the differences between me and my brother as well as the constant hurt feelings that make it hard to communicate with my ex-wife, even after all those years. Can't wait for the day when the dream house will be finished! It will be such a blessing. But you know, Linda, we shouldn't let those problems get too close to our heart. It's not good for our soul, believe me. There are so many expectations that children and relatives might have, and sad to say, often they are not even thankful for the things we do for them. And when it comes to the things we don't do for them, they totally lack understanding for our point of view. It's always just about them! What *we* want, they couldn't care less …

As for now I prefer to be just with the two children I own, but some day they will own themselves, and who knows what will be then. If I take a look at my oldest son, it doesn't give me much hope for the future.

Nowadays children break away from traditional values.

You know, it's kind of frustrating. In the past we had so little. When I was their age, most children were not even able to go to school, and many kids were sitting in class unable to concentrate because they were hungry. Nowadays we send them to school, equipped with all kinds of fancy items like unbreakable pencils, and erasers that look like toys, and of course they get to bring delicious snacks for lunch. And still they complain that they don't like the food in their lunch box and whatever they have, they always want something else and something better, and good is never good enough.

It's hard for me to understand these modern times. I know this makes me sound so old, but really, there are many things which I just can't understand anymore.

I love you Linda!!

I didn't mean to talk in such a bitter way, but at times I can't help it. As I said before, one has to be very careful not to get into that topic too much. It isn't good for our heart and soul!! It really isn't!!

Take care!
Love,
Stephen

12th of December 2011
Dear Stephen,

Don't feel bad about the way you feel. I guess we can't change the way we feel because our feelings are not inherently under our control. They just pop up in response to whatever we experience in our environment and in relation to how much life meets our expectations or fails to do so.

But as you said: The trick is, not to allow those negative feelings to get too permanently present in our heart! It's better for our soul to focus on the good things. You can always find yourself something to look forward to. Like meeting a friend. Or taking a journey. Or living in the dream house, some day.

It's hard for today's children and youngsters to imagine how we lived in their age, and often they don't even want to know. It's not relevant to them how things used to be in the past. They have enough problems of their own to tackle, problems, often brought about by our modern times. Problems which *we* never had to deal with in the past.

Christmas is such a time that stirs up past anguish and frustration, isn't it? The only good thing: It will pass … So let's not get too much involved …

By the way, how is the brown puppy? I haven't heard about him for a while.

Hear from you soon.
Linda

13th of December 2011
Dear Linda,

Thanks for changing the subject. Well, the brown one is already quite sturdy in the meantime. Already interacting a bit more with the environment. Penny doesn't mind if the kids take him. She seems to enjoy a break from mothering the little darling at times anyway. But if it takes too long, she suddenly gets up from the sofa and demands him back. She is a good and watchful mother after all. I have to get up at 3am tomorrow to make it to the private hospital, since I will have to take the community bus. As you know, my money situation is a bit tight right now, so I lack cash for another necessary repair desperately needed for my bike. Well, it's an old bike, so what can you expect! But I'm thankful to have it. It often saves me a lot of time and nerves when going places. Not being able to use it will just make me appreciate it even more, as soon as it works again. Maybe sometimes it's good for us not to have certain things available for a while. We shouldn't take anything for granted. Everything we have could be away again in the future. If anything happened to the world, let's say, for example a bigger disaster like a comet hitting the earth or if the satellites were destroyed because of some gravity shifts or whatever, we suddenly might have to do again without internet and cell phones. I just hope and pray that this will never happen. It would be so depressing. Like being dumped back into utter darkness. Those modern means of communication have brought so much joy into our lives and so many possibilities that we never had in the past. You know, to us here in Africa it means even more because we don't have so many other possibilities. We cannot travel like you people in Europe. We don't have so many facilities available that are within our reach. So it just means so much that we can connect to the entire world in the blink of an eye by internet. It's really a miracle which we never should stop valuing. We could have never met, Linda, without the internet, and knowing you has made my life so much more beautiful! We have to be so thankful!

I really have to sleep now.
Have a good-night-kiss.
Love,
Stephen

14th of December 2011
My dear Stephen,

I'm so glad to hear that the brown puppy is fine and growing. The children will be so happy to keep him. That sure will be a very special Christmas surprise. I think no toy and no game from the shop could surpass this.

Hope your bike can be repaired soon and it is not too complicated to do without it. I admire you for getting up that early. I can well imagine that it must be tough!!
Anyway, have a beautiful day at work!

Yours,
Linda

15th of December 2011
Dear Linda,

This morning during my ride into town I've seen the most beautiful sunrise, and it just made me wish so hard you were here too that it hurt. I just missed you so incredibly much! But, of course I know, I shouldn't be so impatient. In only one and a half months we will meet anyway. You already have your visa, so nothing can get between us now anymore. Just once in a while there comes such a moment when I feel I can't wait any longer. Till now we've counted the month, in a fortnight we will already count the weeks and in the end the days. Seeing you will

be my Christmas. There is nothing I've been waiting for so eagerly in a long time.
Really: You are my very special Christmas gift!

Love,
Stephen

16th of December
Oh Stephen!

What a sweet thing to say! You are such a special person and even more special to me. I would have definitely enjoyed being there with you to see that sunrise. I love both sunrise and sunset. I love nature altogether. And I agree with you. Meeting in Accra will be for both of us our true delayed Christmas present.

Love,
Linda

17th of December 2011
Dear Linda,

If only you knew how much you mean to me! I'm working all around the clock with hardly any time to sleep. I come home exhausted every day, and I have hardly any energy left for my children. I usually bring along some street food which we share with Penny. Then I write a few words to you before I fall asleep on the couch, next to Penny and her little one. My daughter sometimes snuggles up with us which I enjoy very much. My son is already in an age where he doesn't like to cuddle anymore. At least not with me or his sister. I still remember when they both were little and always came running toward me when I came home from work. And how they jumped up on me, and I lay down with one on each side. Those days are gone, and I can't get over how quickly they've grown bigger.

Linda, I'm sorry, but my back hurts so much. I have to lie down and rest.
Take care of yourself!

Love and kisses,
Stephen

17th of December 2011
Dear Stephen,

I hope you feel better soon. You just work too much.
I can understand what you mean talking about the kids. Lori and Kate used to come to my room every day together to kiss me good-night. And at some point they started not coming anymore every day. Once in a while they still do it. But often not. And I have to admit I miss it. Little children have such a pure and direct way of showing their affection.

Well, I also have a lot to do right now which is good because as soon as the Christmas holidays start, nobody has time for language lessons anyway. So it's important that a bit of money comes in beforehand, in order to compensate for the Christmas time. You know, the way things are set up here, practically all people have money at Christmas. Most people receive a double income for Christmas and even retirees receive a double payment in December. Just in my case this month brings only half of my normal monthly income since nobody orders lessons between December 23rd and January 7th. From what I've heard they give people so much money because they want them to consume as much as possible. And all of this consumption is supposed to bring a positive balance to many local businesses which otherwise would finish the year with red figures.

Anyway, please take care of your health!
Love,
Linda

18th of December 2011
Dear Linda,

It was interesting to hear about double incomes for Christmas. Never heard about anything like that. Amazing!! Why do the other people get this and you not? I don't quite understand. This is all very new and different to me.
In the meantime I've bought a nice box, and I plan to hide a card with a picture of the puppy in there for the children. And on the other side of the card it says," Dear David and Mary, I am so happy that I am allowed to stay at your house for good. I couldn't imagine anywhere else I'd rather be. I'm really happy to be your Christmas Puppy!" And besides I also got a pretty, golden ribbon to fix up the present properly and along with it a few sweets for decoration.
What do you think about it?
Love, Stephen

19th of December 2011
Dear Stephen,

What a cute idea! I'm sure they will love it. I've also bought all kinds of presents for the children who will celebrate with me. I still have to think about what to cook. Not so easy with my family because most of us are vegetarians. So the traditional Christmas dishes like sausages or fish are not for us. Here many people buy a carp for Christmas and they sell them even alive. Some let it swim in their bathtub for a day or two before they finally kill and eat it on Christmas Eve. Well, that's definitely not for me. I don't even go along with buying a Christmas tree. I've heard that Christmas trees were originally a heathen custom. By now they have become a Christian tradition around here, which, to me, makes no sense. It's supposed to be about celebrating the tree of life since those pine trees stay also green in winter while most plants here are waiting for their revival in spring. How ridiculous can you get! You celebrate the tree of life by killing a tree!!! Because all those Christmas trees will be thrown away, shortly after Christmas. That's why I never liked them. I just used to take a big pot plant and decorated it with lots of sweets.

Best wishes for your last Christmas preparations.
Linda

20th of December 2011
Dear Linda,

What a special idea to have a live plant for a Christmas tree! It's an interesting philosophical thought: To kill a tree in order to celebrate the tree of life!! There is something to it. Well, you always have very interesting thoughts, and I feel honoured that you share them with me. You still haven't told me about why you don't get a double income for Christmas and most other people do. In case you don't want to talk about it, please forgive me for asking a second time. But the whole topic is pretty "exotic" to me.

Love,
Stephen

21st of December 2011
Dear Stephen,

Well, I'm not offended about your question. Just forgot to answer it somehow. Ok, if you are a freelancer you don't get an extra income. But if you have any kind of employed work or a pension, you do.

In the meantime I've decided for a vegetable pie and a mixed salad. And some ice cream and cake for dessert. Doesn't sound too special, I'm afraid. But at least everybody likes it. Well, I'll buy a few special vegetables for the salad like asparagus and artichokes, black and green olives, and tiny little pickled baby onions and corn on the cab. And I'll buy a variety of ice cream so everybody can eat as much of it as they please.
What are you going to eat for Christmas?

Love,
Linda

22nd of December 2011
Dear Linda,

Don't worry about your menu. It sounds great!

As for us, we don't have any special Christmas dish. I'm not much of a cook, and around here there are no special Christmas dishes. We'll just order some chicken and fufu I guess. Or I'll give the children a choice of what to eat and just order it then.
Don't get too busy with preparations. ☺
Love,
Stephen

23rd of December 2011
Dear Linda

I don't know how to start, but something unexpected has come up today. Sad to say, but the brown puppy has died. I don't quite understand how this could happen. He seemed fine. Must be he caught some disease. Many dogs die here of distemper. Penny even gets a yearly shot for this, but the little one was not vaccinated yet. I guess it was my fault. I've worked so much lately, so I didn't have the time to observe the dogs as much as I should have. That's why I didn't notice in time something was wrong. If I had seen it earlier, I could have taken him to the vet, and maybe they could have saved him. Would have cost a fortune, but I would have done it, I guess.

Well, Christmas is definitely ruined. It was anyway planned to be very modest, but at least the puppy was supposed to be the special present and the centre of it all. Now I have a box and a card and ribbons, but nothing to put inside. The children don`t know it yet. They are visiting their mother for two days right now. It will be horrible when they come back.

Penny was looking for her baby for hours. After I had taken him out to the yard, she wanted to go out there too. So I locked her up in the house and brought the dead little body somewhere further away so she cannot smell him anymore. By now she has settled down on the sofa again, and she isn't reacting to anything I say to her.

I don't know what to do now. I feel guilty. I'm a horrible dog owner and a horrible parent. I love my children and Penny so much, and yet I wasn't even able to keep this tiny little puppy save and alive for them. They both will miss him so much!

Hope at your house everybody is fine.

Love,
Stephen

24th of December 2011
Dear Stephen,

Oh no!! I feel so upset that I don't even know what to say … I'm so sorry that it all came out that way. And I feel kind of frustrated because I know that whatever I could say, it will unfortunately not change a thing. Even though I wish so much that my words could in whatever way make a difference. But whatever I could say, it will not be comforting right now. The only thing I wish to assure you of is that my genuine compassion is with you.
I was really hoping for you and your family to have a nice Christmas. I know it means a lot to

you because you are religious. As for me, Christmas needn't exist. In recent days I already feel a certain well known melancholy creeping up which I call the "Christmas Depression". It's such a time when everything that isn't going well in your life is coming down on you. And each year the weight of it all increases, and it's already getting too much. Too much weight for one person. Too much weight for one life.

I feel so totally empty and burned out. And I know that in this condition I cannot be of any help or inspiration to anybody anyway. So I kindly ask – and I hope that this will be ok with you – that we take a break in writing until those Christmas Holidays are over. My negative feelings will pass, don't worry about me, please. You need not give it a second thought. It's the same every year. Once work starts again and I am busy, everything will be fine. So let's just take a break until the 7th of January!

Then things will be different. Christmas will be over and we can seriously start looking forward to seeing each other. By then there will be only three weeks and a couple of days left! Isn't that exciting?

And don't think that you are a bad parent and a bad dog owner. You are a kind and caring person. That's why you feel like that. And there was probably nothing you could have done about it. It

161

just happened in an extremely inappropriate moment (not that there could be an appropriate moment for such things to happen). But still, this situation with Christmas at hand makes it of course even worse.

I would feel silly wishing you a "Merry Christmas" knowing that under the given circumstances, there is no chance for this Christmas to be "merry". So I won't do it.
But I wish for all of us a promising and wonderful NEW YEAR, full of love and joy and thrilling experiences ahead.

Take care and be assured of my love.
I'll be back with you on the 7th of January.
Love,
Linda

24th of December 2011
Dear Linda,

Thanks for your kind words. I'm sorry that Christmas seems to be such a complicated time for you altogether. I even feel bad about adding to your burdens. Wish I could have some more joyful news to share at a time like this.

But whatever: Life will go on, and there are better things ahead. Let's just take care of our situation the best we can and meet again online on the 7th of January. The year to come will be our year. It will forever be the year when we first met in person!! Isn't that exciting?

All my love

Stephen

31st of December 2011

Dear Linda,

Just now I see some fireworks over the town of Accra, and I can't help thinking of you. I truly miss you. Can't wait for the 7th to come.

Best wishes for you and your family.

Love

Stephen

P.S.: I don't expect an answer before the 7th of January

7th of January 2012
Dear Stephen,

Thank you so much for your good wishes for the New Year.

Today I worked again for the first time, and I'm busy again and feeling a lot better. It's always such a relief when this time is over. Now there is still my birthday to come on the 10th of this month. Once this day has passed, everything will be fine. I don't remember if I have mentioned this to you or not. But around my birthday, unfortunate things tend to happen. I always thought that my birthday brings bad luck. Just like the fact that I was born brought an unfortunate turn to my mother's life. My grandmother had a stroke on my birthday, and my father's funeral was also on my birthday. So I came to the conclusion that my birthday somehow brings bad luck and stopped celebrating it. But still I get nervous around this time, and I'm always happy when this date has passed.

Might sound stupid but I just can't help feeling in that apprehensive way.

Hugs and kisses,
Linda

8th of January 2012
Oh Linda!

How can you believe something like that? How
could your birthday ever be a sign of bad luck!
You are such a wonderful person and I can assure you that this world is a better and a more
beautiful place because you are here. Don't worry! Of course, if something unfortunate happens
exactly on your birthday, one can feel tempted to
believe in some kind of "bad luck" connected to
that day. But this is definitely just a coincidence.
Hey! I thought you are the one from the modern
scientifically minded country that doesn't believe
in such things like curses and superstitions. ☺

By the way, in the meantime I have reserved
your room at the Grand View Hotel. With bathtub as you wished. If you want anything specific
at the hotel room, please feel free to tell me, but
tell me in time because it might take a while for
me to organise it. I will definitely do my best.
After all, I want you to feel good in my country.

By now, the children have come to accept the
facts concerning the loss of the puppy. They
were really sweet about not getting any Christmas presents this year. You know, they tried to
cheer me up by telling me it didn't matter. But
we agreed that someday in the future when Pen-

ny will have puppies again, we will keep our favourite. And we will make him a little house out of that big Christmas box.

Hope to hear from you soon.
Yours always
Stephen
P.S.: I attach the hotel reservation

9th of January 2012
Dear Stephen,

You can be so proud of your children!!
And the idea to plan on keeping a future puppy sounds like a very good one.
I was already wondering how you guys had been doing, but in my first mail after Christmas I didn't dare to ask for details so as not to trigger that whole emotional context again.

Thanks for the hotel reservation. Wow! Soon I will have to think about packing my suitcase. By the way, is there anything specific that I could bring from my country?

Love
Linda

10th of January 2012
HAPPY BIRTHDAY LINDA

Hope you are having a wonderful day, and I pray
that all your uneasy feelings that you had beforehand are now away. Enjoy life to the fullest! You
deserve it, my love!
I'm sure you are busy today, so I don't want to
take your time.

You are forever in my heart and on my mind.
Yours,
Stephen

13th of January 2012
What's wrong Linda?
I have not received any mail from you in the past
days. What is going on? I start to get worried, so
please write.
Yours,
Stephen

15th of January
Where are you Linda?
My heart feels heavy and burdened because I
don't know what has happened. Yet there is

nothing I can do but wait. I feel like I'm going crazy with fear. Please write. Please!
Stephen

17th of January 2012
Dear Stephen,

I'm so extremely sorry that I didn't write back. But the things that happened in my close sur- roundings were so overwhelming that they left me practically speechless.
I don't know where to start, but I'll try to ex- plain:
Well, on my birthday (thanks so much for your kind wishes) I came to Kate's room in the even- ing, and I saw that she had lit a candle on the table. It looked dangerous to me because the wick was kind of long already and the flame therefore huge and most of all, close to the can- dle there were some bags hanging on the wall which in my opinion could easily catch fire. So I told her not to do that and pointed out what all could happen with such a big flame that isn't properly secured.

So far my birthday had been a nice day. Every- body had given me a present and tried to make me feel good. But when I talked to Kate about this candle, she suddenly snapped and got really nasty again. She kind of ridiculed my words and acted again in that disrespectful way she has lately adopted when talking to *me*. The end of it was that she put out the flame. But the way she had talked to me kind of ruined it, and I ended up crying secretly in my room.

You know, her behaviour just really hurts me.

Next day it seems Kate didn't go to school. I don't know if I have told you, but one day a week she has to go to school for theoretical lessons. In the afternoon someone rang at our door, and there was a girl who, to my surprise, delivered some school materials for Kate. Later that day it turned out that Kate hadn't been to school at all, and this girl had just brought her all the sheets and homework assignments that had been handed out. Well, actually Kate had spent the day at home, mostly sleeping in her bed, and I hadn't noticed it. She had done a good job fooling me, by removing her jacket and her boots from the hall. She hid her outdoor clothes in the children's room in a place where I couldn't see them, and she herself was up on the loft bed. This bed is an excellent hiding place because even if someone enters the room, it's impossible to see what is up there unless you actually climb up the ladder. Now, if I assume that Kate is in school, there is of course no reason to do so.

You can imagine how surprised I was when, in the evening, Kate all of a sudden came down from the loft bed. I realised that she had obviously skipped school, but there was nothing I could do about it anymore.

Later that night I went to bed rather early. I was already sound asleep when suddenly I could hear some screaming. I woke up a bit disorientated and thought, "My god, why are these children fighting again!" Since the screaming didn't stop, I forced myself to crawl out of bed and headed towards the children's room. As I passed by the kitchen, I couldn't believe my eyes. Kate was standing there, and the upper part of her body was in flames. She had turned on the water in the kitchen sink and kept pouring it over her hands. Obviously she was in a state of shock and unaware that the flames had already caught onto the whole front side of her shirt.

I just stared at her for a moment. Frozen. Unable to believe. Then, in the next moment, I ran to the bathroom. I grabbed a wet towel and desperately tried to extinguish the fire. In between the phone rang, but I had no time to pick it up. When the fire was finally out, I urged Kate to quickly cool her body with cold water in the bathtub. Then I inspected her for damage. On the belly there was a huge area that looked pretty alarming to me, so I called the ambulance. In the meantime, the phone rang again several times. This was Clarissa who, as it turned out later, had been on the phone with Kate when the whole trouble started. But she couldn't guess what was going on. From her point of position she had been in casual conversation with her sister when Kate suddenly started to scream in panic, and then the call was interrupted. Poor Clarissa tried to dial again several times but nobody picked up anymore. She tried to reach me but couldn't. So, of course, she got extremely worried and phoned the ambulance. Yet, in this agitating situation, the exact address of my new flat had suddenly slipped her mind. Because of this, there was nothing the ambulance could do. Clarissa already considered rushing over to my place by taxi when I could finally call her back. While I was waiting for the ambulance, we exchanged our info on what had happened.

Well, it turned out that Kate had lit that candle again despite my warnings the day before. When she wanted to take some notes during the call with her sister, she reached over to get a pen. And while doing so, her shirt caught fire.

By the way, at a certain moment when we were still in the bath, it suddenly struck me that this candle might still be on. So I raced back to that room just in time because several items on the table had already caught fire. I ran back to the bathroom to get another wet towel, and after

171

some efforts I luckily managed to put out the flames.

When the ambulance arrived, they decided to take us to a nearby hospital. Just as we were leaving the house, Kate suddenly remembered that she had put some food into the oven. Oh my god, just think of it!! If she had forgotten about it (which could have happened very easily in the hectic situation at hand) this could have led to another fire and Lori and Cora might have died in their sleep from smoke poisoning while we were away in the hospital for hours. On our return home, we might not have had a home anymore! And in such an incident the household insurance wouldn't pay either. They pay the loss on other people's property but not the damage that is done to your own flat. Just thinking about it is too much. My god! How you can lose everything so easily in one unfortunate moment! We can be incredibly thankful that we are all still alive and that our home is still standing. Of course, Kate has a bigger injury, but also in her case, if I had woken up a few minutes later or if I hadn't been home to help her, she would have died in the fire.

Anyway, in the hospital that doctor in charge was a bit stupid, and she acted like it was not so bad after all. That it probably looked more dramatic than it actually was and that it would all heal more or less by itself with the help of some cream that she applied. Days later it finally turned out that this big greenish-pale area in the middle of the red one wasn't, as the Doctor thought, an undamaged area but a place with third degree burns! This became clear when after several days a huge blister bulged out. So now the state of the art is that Kate will need an operation where they are going to transplant some skin from her thigh to this place on the belly. Otherwise, they fear this wound could change into coarse scar tissue which might make it hard to move without pain when bending or stretching. So we are waiting now for the hospital to set a date. In the meantime they send her to lots of places to get all kinds of check-ups needed before surgery. To the lab for a blood-screen, to a heart specialist and for a lung x-ray, and all of them have to give their ok before the operation can finally be given approval. All this is connected to long ways getting to doctor's offices, lining up there and waiting – when actually Kate should really be given a chance to get a lot of rest and stay in bed. Now, today she came home crying from some doctor's place, and I think she has a fever. No wonder! If it gets worse, I will take her back to the hospital because this could be an infection developing in the open wound.

Oh yes, and I still haven't told you that Lori and Cora didn't even wake up in that night when the "big action" took place. I really wonder how they managed to keep on sleeping next to all that screaming! So the following day it was quite a shocking surprise to Lori when she was told the facts in detail. She almost felt bad about not waking up!

I have to stop writing now, but I will keep you updated as soon as there are any "breaking news".

Yours,
Linda

18th of January 2012
Oh my god, Linda!!

What a story. And again something like that happened so close to your birthday! Unbelievable! I hope and pray that your daughter will recover soon without any permanent damage remaining. Children are so reckless in this age. They never listen to us when we tell them that something might be dangerous. What an unfortunate thing to happen!!
Please, Linda, take good care of yourself, and don't forget to eat enough!
Take care
Stephen

19th of January 2012
Dear Stephen,

I am so utterly sorry, but I have to inform you that I am not any at all sure that I can come to Accra as arranged. There are only twelve days left until my flight, scheduled for the 31st of January, and I don't know what will happen till then. As I told you already two nights ago, Kate suddenly developed a fever. I have to say that I'm not exactly surprised considering all this running around with the open wound. So I decided yesterday to take her back to the hospital ambulance, and I told them my opinion on how this is all quite counterproductive. The end of it was that they kept her there. Due to the fact that she already has an infection building up in this wound, they will move her up on the surgery list, and the operation is now scheduled already for the 21st of this month. I believe this is basically good news, but I cannot guarantee for anything. First everything needs to be under full control here before I can consider going away. You are a father yourself, so I am sure you understand. But of course, I would be very sad if we should have to cancel my flight.

Love,
Linda

20th of January 2012
Dear Linda,

Of course I understand that your daughter's health is first priority. But this doesn't change the fact that I am devastated by the thought that our long awaited meeting in person might now all of a sudden not happen. I have to confess that over the past months the idea of seeing you soon here in Accra, was the one thing I've been living up to. Feels like my whole emotional backup is crumbling down to dust right now.

Oh Linda! I hope and pray that things will still work out.

For tomorrow, I wish your daughter the best for her surgery. May the angels of the Lord be around her and lead the hands of the surgeon. I will pray for her tomorrow.

Linda, you are so close to my heart!

Love,
Stephen

21st of January 2012
Dear Stephen,

Seems like the surgery was performed with success. Of course, afterwards Kate didn't feel fine. She had never been operated before, and I guess she is not tolerating the anaesthesia too well. I wasn't there, right at the moment when she woke up, because I had to work, and besides, she had anyway asked Clarissa to be with her. By the time I arrived, Clarissa was just about to leave. She told me that Kate had been vomiting for hours, time and again. And that she was still feeling pretty sick. Of course, she also has pain, but this is normal. So let's hope for the best.
Stephen, I can't go on writing right now. I just feel so totally wiped out.
Thanks for always being on my side.
Love,
Linda

22nd of January 2012
Dear Linda,

I'm very relieved to hear that things went more or less fine. Of course, it will take time for her to heal. But she is young and basically in good

health. So she should be able to recover within a reasonable amount of time.
My love and good wishes are with you always.
Love,
Stephen

23rd of January 2012
Dear Stephen,

Actually there is nothing new today. Everything according to circumstances. I'm just a bit finished.
Love,
Linda

24th of January 2012
Dear Linda,

I'm glad to hear that everything is progressing in the right direction. It's no surprise that you feel finished. It's been a very stressful and exhausting time for you. It's amazing how emotional stress can make the body so tired. But I know....
I give you all my strength.
Love you!
Steve

25th of January 2012
Dear Stephen,

Today I spoke to the doctor and the plan is that Kate can go home already by the end of the week. To be exact, on the 29th. I have to talk to Clarissa about the whole issue tomorrow. Because I need to find out whether she thinks it's ok that I go away and if she feels capable of handling. We will see. But altogether that's good news!
Love,
Linda

26th of January 2012
Oh Linda, my love!

Does this mean that there is still hope that you will actually come? I didn't even dare to ask about it in the past days. I try not to get too excited, but I can hardly keep my emotions down.
Oh Linda, this situation is almost too hard to handle for me.
Looking forward to your next mail.

Yours,
Stephen

27th of January 2012
Dear Stephen,

I don't wish to keep you waiting a single minute longer concerning the news I have about my journey. I've talked to my daughter and she said that it was all the same to her; she had anyway planned on taking care of the kids and already made arrangements to have more time for them. So, there is actually no big difference whether I'm here or not, now that everything is under control.

And this means that I can confirm my arrival on the 31st of January at 11:35 pm at Accra airport. My god! I can hardly believe it. That's in only four days!! Of course, I'm a bit worried to leave the situation here in someone else's hands. But Clarissa is grown-up and very reliable, and she has my full trust.

By the way, what should I pack? How is the weather at this time?

Love,
Linda

28th of January 2012
Dear Linda,

You cannot imagine how overwhelmed with joy I am. Finally my heart's dream will actually come true. I thank you. And I thank the Lord.

Talking about the weather: We still have here a condition called "harmatan" which is a very dry wind that makes the lips break open if you don't cream them enough. It also causes the skin to be abnormally dry and scaly. Usually at this time of the year harmatan should already be over, but this year it seems to stretch out a bit longer. Besides, it is expected to be very hot and sunny.
I will also go and arrange everything at your hotel room to make sure you have enough food there. What should I buy for you? Please tell me before your departure, so I can still arrange things.
Love always,
Stephen

29th of January 2012
Dear Stephen,

Thanks for your info. Don't worry too much about food. What I'd care to have most is some nice tropical fruit. I always carry along a water-cooker because I want to have tea in the room at any time I please, day or night! Of course, I will also bring a large variety of teabags, and we can change the hotel room into a private teahouse ☺

Can't wait for sharing the first cup of tea together there.

Love,
Linda

30th of January 2012
Dear Carla,

I enjoyed our long phone call yesterday very much. Thanks for your sympathy.

There is something I wanted to ask you. As you know, I am going to Accra to see this internet friend of mine. And as much as I trust that everything will be fine, I would definitely feel safer if we could communicate every day as long as I am there. Despite of all the mails we have exchanged, it is a given fact that I don't know this man. And of course, anything could happen. What do you think about it?
Linda

30th of January 2012
Dear Linda,

Actually I was quite worried about your trip to Accra. And I agree it's a good idea to stay in touch. I can be your personal security service. ☺ But if I don't hear anything from you for longer than a day, what should I do then? My god, I really hope nothing will happen.

Carla

30th of January 2012
Dear Carla,

Thank you so much!!
Well, you have my number. I also send you Stephen's numbers, both, private and from work, as an SMS to your phone. So, if you suddenly don't hear anything from me and cannot reach me on the phone, try to contact him. If you cannot get in touch with both of us or if you can reach only him and something seems fishy, call the police in Austria or the Embassy of Ghana in Switzerland. I guess, they will tell you where to turn to, or maybe they will contact the authorities in Ghana directly.

Oh Gosh! This sounds all so negative and serious! Actually I really hope to spend a few nice and exciting days there. I really like Stephen very much. He seems to be a valuable character, and I hope everything turns out fine.

So you will hear from me on a daily basis all my exciting news directly from Accra!

Thanks again,

Linda

30th of January 2012

Ok, Linda,

Everything clear. I wish you a wonderful time in Ghana, and please come back safe and healthy.

P.S.: I won't have time and inspiration to write but a few lines because right now I have a lot of stress at work. So, there won't be anything interesting to tell from my side.

But I can assure you, in case of emergency I will take action. And of course, I will enjoy reading all your interesting stories about Ghana!! So please, tell me all about it in detail. Just don't be mad if my answers are rather blunt and short. We are not in the same situation right now …

Hope you understand.

Carla

30th of January 2012
My beloved Linda,

This will be my last mail before we see each other. I still wish you a pleasant flight and a wonderful journey. My heart is already going crazy, and I' m sure I won't be able to sleep tonight. I'm too excited.
See you tomorrow at the airport!!
Can't wait anymore!

Love
Stephen

30th of January 2012
Dear Stephen,

I'm already expecting my taxi to pick me up in a few minutes. So this is my last mail until we meet at the airport as appointed. Keep it together and try to sleep a bit. Sleeping will shorten the countdown of those few hours that are still between us.
I' m already very excited myself.

Love,
Linda

1st of February, at 2am
Dear Carla,

It was almost midnight when I finally had collected my suitcase and directed myself to the exit. After the usual formalities like customs and visa control, I finally passed the glass door that leads to the arrival hall. I was surprised to see that the plastic casing of my suitcase was sweating immensely, the water was practically running down from it. There were lots of people standing there who were all awaiting someone. Taxi drivers approached me, offering a lift to my hotel. I told them that I was waiting for someone. As I was standing there, I noticed that quite a few people were watching me very attentively. I felt excited and a bit uneasy at the same time, hoping that Stephen would show up soon. It was dark in the hall and my eyes couldn't really make out anything. I tried to recall Stephen's face, the way I remembered it from pictures …

You know, just before I left, I had ordered a new pair of glasses, something professional from the optician, not those cheap ones from the China-Shop which I have used so far. Now, believe it or not, as I put on those new glasses to read the board with the departure flights, those spectacles just fell apart. One of these tiny screws had come off, and of course, no chance to find it again. So now I can only use them while holding the broken side with my right hand. Isn't that stupid!! As if it weren't enough, I had to check in at the machine myself, and this flight attendant refused to help me at first. Finally, after several futile attempts, she dismissively stepped beside me to take action. She really made a big thing out of it, stating several times that this was not her job and my broken glasses not her fault; and my poor eyes and lack of computer literacy none of her business. When I finally had boarding passes for both flights, I went ahead for hand luggage control and put my watch inside the box as always. After I had passed the control, I picked up my items and guess what!! My watch was missing!! I reported this to the officials and they even stopped the x-ray box and looked inside, but the watch was gone. Someone must have stolen it! So, before even entering the plane, I already had no glasses and no watch anymore. Incredible!!

Ok, back to Accra …
Finally, after a few guys who turned out not to be Stephen (but acted like they were waiting there, only for me) my friend showed up. He quickly said something that sounded rather unfriendly to the guy who was talking to me at that time. Then Stephen turned towards me. We looked at each other, both a bit shy. Then he said, "Welcome to Ghana! Welcome to our poor country!" He took

my suitcase and we headed towards a taxi. On the ride to the hotel we were both quiet. After he showed me the room, we still talked a bit, but I soon asked him to leave because I was very tired. So we have arranged to meet tomorrow, at 11am.

Besides, I have delicious fruit in my room and a laptop which I can use for the whole week. So everything is fine.
I'll be back with you in the late evening.
Linda

1st of February, at 8 am

Hi Linda,
Glad to hear that you have arrived fine.
I expect to hear from you again tonight.
Carla

1st of February, at 11 pm

Hi Carla,
I am fine. Today Stephen picked me up at 11am. He was on time and wore a nice African shirt. First thing he gave me a shawl for a present. You know, this kind that looks like those banners

people wave at football stadiums with the name of their team on it. He had ordered it from a local friend who makes such items. It's hand-woven, and it says on it: Welcome to Ghana, Linda. From what he said it's a tradition to give something like that to a visitor as a gift of appreciation.

Stephen had decided to play tourist guide, and we left the hotel together. At first we went to the Kwame Nkrumah Mausoleum which seems to be a place he is quite proud of. I took a look and listened to his words of explanation about how Kwame Nkrumah had been the first president of Ghana and therefore a great national hero. We took several pictures inside the tomb, and it was nice and cool there. Later we strolled along some street that led to the so-called Independence Arch. After taking some photographs there, we still went to the National Museum and later to Memorial Park. I was glad to sit down a bit on the grass and rest. A woman came by and sold some ice-cream. The funny thing was that this ice-cream was packed in tubes, you know kind of like tubes for toothpaste with a plastic cover that you can screw of, and then you just press the tube and the ice cream comes out like toothpaste too. It was just regular vanilla ice cream, nothing special taste-wise, but the presentation was interesting. We also bought some water. Guess what, they sell water here in small plastic bags!! You see everywhere people with a large tray balanced on their heads, and they have a big pyramid of those little plastic bags draped on the tray. Along with the bag you get a straw, and Stephen showed me how you just punch a small hole next to the place where the bag is tied with a knot. It took me a while to get used to it, and at first I spilled quite a bit of water. But in the meantime I manage to drink out of such wobbly packages!

As we went back, we still talked a bit in the hotel room. We had tea and some mango that tasted amazing. We spoke about all the places he plans to bring me to, and it is sweet to see how much he tries to please me.

After he went home, I still tried to get a bit more organised in the room. Obviously they save electricity by equipping the rooms with very dim light. And I really have a problem because of my broken glasses. I will never again travel without packing at least one extra pair. Since it was really hard for me to find things in my suitcase, I tried to place every item in an appropriate place. But I'm still going in circles every time I want to use something.

Actually the GRAND VIEW HOTEL has turned out to be a "no view hotel" for me. My room is on the second floor, and it doesn't really have a window. I mean on one side there is a window, but it only leads to the hall, and part of the view is covered by a wall. On the other side there is the elevator and I have to keep the heavy curtain closed, or else, people waiting for the elevator could look straight into my room. Well, if I open a small slit of the curtain and put my head right next to the window pane, then I can see a small section of a window that is located at the end of the hallway. And from there I can actually watch a small area of the street. It's too bad that I don't have a proper window because it would be very interesting for me to sit up there and watch all this busy, bustling life in the streets of Accra. It could be very special to observe all this activity down there, without people noticing you.

I don't understand why Stephen didn't get me a better room somewhere higher up and with the advertised great view. Guess he doesn't really understand what is important for me, to feel well. For example, the bathtub. I mean, I do have a room with a bathtub, but this tub doesn't have a plug. I understand that this is a method of saving water because that way people cannot take baths. Ok, another item to pack in the future! Plugs for bathtubs in different sizes! As for the moment, I have to improvise. I searched around amongst my cosmetics and found a shampoo cover which almost completely fits. So I stuffed a plastic bag into the drain and fixed it with the shampoo cover. I have to say this construction works well enough to facilitate a nice warm bath to relax and get really clean. I always feel that taking a shower doesn't really produce this deep clean sensation that you experience after soaking in a bathtub. And most of all I miss the relaxing effect.

Well, at least this problem is solved for now. I'm glad I found a solution because I don't want to mention anything about it to Stephen. I don't want to sound like I'm complaining about every little detail. I guess it's hard to explain the importance of bathtubs to someone who has never had one in his own house. You don't miss what you don't know.

For me a bath is such a simple way to improve my general well-being. It just makes me feel better instantly. So why should I do without it?!

Well Carla, thanks for listening to me. I will be with you again tomorrow night.
Linda

2nd of February, at 8 am
Dear Linda,

I'm glad to hear that things are basically fine in your place. I really enjoy listening to you.
Yours,
Carla

2nd of February, at 11 pm
Dear Carla,

I'm a little tired because every morning I receive
a phone call from the reception at 7 am. "Breakfast is ready in the dining hall", says the voice of
some girl.
Well, actually I'm not interested in this breakfast, and I already told them yesterday they need
not bother to phone me. But they keep calling!

I had another more serious problem to sort out.
Unfortunately there is no safe in the room, and I
definitely felt a bit uncomfortable with this situation. I don't want to carry all my valuables with
me all the time. But leaving things in the hotel
room is also no option. Especially: I have 2000
euros with me that are not meant for spending.
This is just emergency money, in case something
goes wrong. For example, if I missed a plane and
had to buy an extra ticket or whatever. Now, here
you can only leave things in the hotel's safe next
to the reception, but in order to do so, you have
to list every single item you deposit there. And I
don't want any of those locals to see that money.
I just don't feel comfortable about it. I also didn't
want Stephen to know. But since I needed his
help in communicating with the man at the front
desk, I just had to explain the issue to him. I
pointed out that this is also to me a lot of money,

and that losing it would be a tremendous problem. I tried to explain to him how important it is that I arrive back home on the appointed day. And that I would lose jobs if I was unable to come back due to whatever circumstances. He acted like he understood, but I saw his eyes glancing at the money. I guess it blew his mind. And of course, I felt pretty uneasy.

Today we went to a place called "Abury Botanical Gardens" that is said to be very beautiful. I was a bit disappointed because most of the area looked pretty dry and barren. But who knows, maybe there is more to see at other times of the year.

Later we took a walk by the sea. There is a beach right next to a slum, frequented mostly by people who live in this neighbourhood. You see children playing there and young men who do sports. Some couples take a walk, and local people offer food and drink. They sell here everywhere banana chips which actually look and taste pretty much like our potato chips. They also have the same yellow colour.

Interesting enough: You see hardly anybody swimming at this beach. Stephen has already told me sometime before that actually most people in Accra cannot even swim! And that it is not possible to go inside the water because until you come back out, your things would be stolen. This of course, makes a lot of sense. So if you don't live in this neighbourhood you can only take a walk there.

As we went back alongside the street, I watched all those porters in surprise. It's incredible how much they can carry on their head. You see men who transport up to seven suitcases on their head, all stacked up one on top of the other like a tower. Amazing! And they do so all day long in this heat! No surprise that many of them look incredibly exhausted and worn-out.

At the same time they also seem to be very religious. Continuously you have all kinds of cars driving by with banners full of bible quotes and loudspeakers that advertise some church. It's pretty obtrusive how they call attention. That's something we are not used to in Europe. I mean, in America you see that too. This more aggressive approach when it comes to promoting religion. This claim to have the right beliefs, and this urge to force them on everyone. When I voiced my surprise, Stephen just proudly stated that Ghana is a Christian country. It's a little bit hard for me to hold back my personal opinion. I don't like it, but, on the other hand, I don't want to be disrespectful.

Sometimes it's almost funny. I took a picture of this one woman who was sitting right next to her little shop with this incredibly grumpy expression on her face. Yet, on the shop it says in huge

capital letters: THE SECRET OF MY JOY IS
JESUS Oh no!! This face didn't reflect any joy!!
But religious people are often like that, according
to my experience. They are hypocrites who rarely practise what they preach.
But I somehow liked the man with the wheelbar-
row on which was written: ALL SHALL PASS

I mean, Stephen told me a few extra facts about
those people you see here in the streets. Most of
these porters actually don't have a home here in
Accra. They come from the countryside and want
to sell here some agricultural products or work as
porters. Many of the women have to sleep unpro-
tected in the streets at night, and it's quite common that they get raped. And many of them end
up pregnant as a consequence of rape. They have
to keep working then until birth because poor
families in the countryside depend on their income. After birth those children are left behind
with family members in their village. And the
women themselves carry on working in town
soon. Of course, this doesn't sound good.

Tomorrow we are going to Cape Coast Castle. It
seems to be a very famous place to visit around
here.

You will hear from me again soon.
Linda

3rd of February, at 7 am

Dear Linda,

I can imagine that many things one sees in such a country are pretty alienating!! But very interesting to hear.
Hope your money will be safe in that hotel safe. I would be scared someone could rob it from me shortly after I pick it up and even mug me on the way to the airport. If they all know about the money, such a robbery can be arranged with a little phone call. So please be careful!

Carla

3rd of February, at 11 pm

Dear Carla,

I have to admit that I share your concern about the money issue, but there is just no better alternative.

Ok, let's talk about Cape Coast Castle.
It was a longer ride to go there, and I enjoyed getting out of the city a bit. When we arrived, one of those street vendors came up to me and

tried to sell me some objects made of shells. I did my best to explain that we are not allowed to bring along such souvenirs inside the European Union nowadays, but he didn't quite understand me. So I explained it to Stephen and urged him to inform the guy because it's really no good if tourists buy those objects but later face problems at customs. As I know that this hassle can range from confiscation of the object to rather high fines, it is definitely a fact those people should know about. They never travel, so they have no idea. Poor guy! I practically felt sorry for him when I saw his face drop during Stephen's explanation. Well, after all we informed him that his business idea was practically leading to something illegal. Must be frustrating to hear, especially if you don't have so many alternatives. Kind of reminded me of a story Clarissa told me about Kenya when she was there the second time. She visited some friend's hometown and his village turned out to be so remote that those people had actually never seen a white face before!! She mentioned that babies even started crying when they saw her!!

Well, his family presented a very special gift for their guest. Guess what it was? It was a chicken!! I mean, a live chicken!! And of course she was expected to take it home! Her friend had to explain in detail that chicken are not allowed on the plane and that it was therefore impossible to take this chicken back home. I think they solved the problem in the end by keeping this chicken there for remembrance of their very special guest. But they insisted that it should be *her* chicken and that they were just taking care of it due to existing circumstances.

You have to consider that in such a Kenyan village people know nothing about the rest of the world. They don't speak English, and they don't even speak Swahili. So, since they only know their local tribal language, the world practically ends at the borderline of their rural settlements.

Well, I would have expected them to be more aware of customs regulations here in Accra. After all, this is a capital with high circulation of visitors from African countries as well as from overseas.

As we went inside the castle there was quite a bit of information on historical facts. Nowadays Cape Coast Castle is visited by many tourists, especially also by African Americans who wish to see the exact place where their ancestors had boarded the ship that brought them to America as slaves.

As you go inside the slave dungeon, you can feel the tragic, burdened atmosphere that has built up in this place over time and still hoovers there like an enormous emotional cloud. You can't avoid your dismay, as you see pictures demonstrating how the slaves were tortured and mistreated. Many of them got sick and died already before shipment. Beautiful female slaves were separated from the rest. They washed and dressed them before they were raped by the guards. If they got pregnant, they were killed and their bodies just thrown away. If they survived until shipping, they at last had to pass THE DOOR OF NO RE-TURN.

Of course, many of them died on the transport. Only the strongest survived long enough that they could finally be sold in America ... While we were shown around, this African American couple were always next to us. I secretly watched them from the corner of my eyes. They couldn't hold back their tears as we moved on from site to site. It must be such an incredibly painful feeling if you are a descendant of those people who actually went through all of this. It must be so burdening for them to stand in that place. But I guess they can be very proud of their ancestors who had survived all of this.

We took quite a few pictures, and by the time we left the castle we were both walking in silence for a longer time. The coast is very beautiful there. We strolled along and watched the fishermen for a while. Then we accessed a small café and relaxed with some refreshments. And we didn't feel like talking for a long time.

On the way back to town we still stopped at a big market area and bought some fruit. My depressive mood recovered somehow when I saw the most amazing mangoes I had ever seen. Increddible! They really had the size of a watermelon!

I was glad that Stephen had to leave right after he had brought me back to the hotel because I felt tired and therefore happy to be alone. I had a lot to think about and took a bath in order to feel better. I prepared some tea and lay down with my feet elevated on a pillow. After I had recovered my senses a bit, I ate one of the mangoes. It tasted amazingly delicious.

I'm already very tired tonight so I will stop writing now.
Have a nice day at work and don't stress yourself too much. ☺

Bye,
Linda

4th of February, at 7 am

Hi Linda,

Glad to hear that everything is fine.
It was very interesting to hear about Cape Coast Castle. I had never heard about it before. I guess, we all don't know that much about Ghana here in Austria.
Thanks for wishing me a nice day. I really have to cut down on working so much every day, or else I will break down or get sick. But right now there is just no way around it.
I have to say it's really nice to read your mails because that way my attention is moved on to something completely different at least for a few moments.
Thanks for sharing your experiences with me.

Love,
Carla

4th of February, at 5 pm

Dear Carla,

Today I'm writing already earlier because Stephen and I are going to visit a night market close to Kwame Nkrumah Circle. I'm really looking forward to seeing that place after having heard about it so often in the past months.

For lunch we went to a restaurant where we ate some local food. And then Stephen wanted to buy me an African dress. I said "no" at first, but he just insisted to do so. I was afraid that I wouldn't be able to find something I liked. Most of the things they have here are not exactly my size. Often also not exactly my colour combination. But then I found a shoulder free dress with a smoked top and the colours are white, gold-ochre and dark-red. African style pattern. The skirt is wide and the length goes down to a little bit under the knee, which is a length I often choose for. I actually really like this dress and I can well imagine wearing it in Austria, too. You know, often those things are nice to wear in the country of origin, but one wouldn't necessarily do so at home.

Stephen was very pleased that I had found something, and he immediately encouraged me to select something for my children too. There was a jumpsuit with wide short pants and a flap, but you know how children are in this age. They are so specific when it comes to clothes. I guess they wouldn't wear something that is fashionable in a faraway country that they haven't been to themselves. Besides, those things are probably not exactly cheap, and I don't want Stephen to spend so much money. I tried to explain, and he looked a bit disappointed at first. But then we found a box with fashion jewellery and got them two bracelets instead. We took a pink one for Lori and a green one for Kate.

When we went back to the hotel room, I told him that I had also brought some gifts for him and his children. Since he hadn't given me any hint about what they would prefer, I had opted for quite a few school things. I tried to find special products with some extra features which they might not have here in Africa. I had some crayons that can make more than one colour at the same time and a few so-called glitter pens which girls usually like very much. Stephen himself got all excited about a pen with golden ink. He decided to keep it for himself. He also stated that his kids would probably fancy the pyramid shaped pencil sharpeners since he had never seen such ones before. He thanked me a lot for the professional calculator, pointing out that it would be an advantage for his son to have it in the upper classes of Secondary School. He was also pleased with the perfume I had given him and thanked me for the big bag of Austrian sweets, chocolates, and treats for Penny.

.

Tomorrow we will go to some national park where there is also a so-called "Canopy Walk". As far as I have understood it, this is a construction of narrow ways that lead from one treetop to the next. It's all made of natural materials, mostly ropes, and just where you walk there are some narrow wooden boards.

Stephen has actually told me weeks ago on the phone that he is afraid of height. So for him, going to this place must be a real challenge. Yet somehow he is totally keen on the idea of going up there together with me. Kind of sweet!

Well, Carla, I have to get ready for the night market now. I'll be back with you tomorrow.

Yours,
Linda

5th of February, at 7 am

Hi Linda,

I'm glad to hear that you are enjoying your time and that things are fine.
I'm sure you will look very interesting in your new African dress. ☺
Take care, Carla

5th of February, at 11 pm

Dear Carla,

What do you mean with "you will look INTER-ESTING in your new African dress"? Are you making fun of me? I know of course that however African I dress, I will never look African. It's not like in Spain. In Spain, just looking at me, people often thought that I am Spanish as long as I didn't talk. But of course, in a place like Ghana I will always stick out as a visible foreigner.

By the way, the night market was pretty cool.
First of all it's a great idea to have a market open at night when temperatures are just perfect. And people who are at work all day, can't go shopping during those regular opening hours.
African markets are always an adventure for your senses. Very colourful, quite loud, and with a rich pool of smells fighting for dominance. Sometimes you can be astonished what kind of articles you might run into. In a globalised world you never know in which corner of the world a certain product might pop up next. To my great surprise they sold there a brand of juice which I always used to buy in Spain. They make juice from pineapple and peach as well as orange and apple and all their products come in tetra pack without any additional sugar added.

I guess people come there to shop as well as to enjoy some snack or drink. I took some fresh coconut and Stephen had a coke. We also ate some very interesting fruit. It actually looks more like a nut, and it is black and feels like velvet. Very unusual. You just put it inside your mouth and let it melt. And when it dissolves, it tastes sweet and aromatic like some kind of a natural candy. But it actually grows exactly the way they sell it there on some tree. I mean it is not dried or candied or modified in any other way. I forgot the name, though, but if we had that in Austria I think I would buy it quite often.

The Canopy Walk was nice, just that you don't see too many of the advertised animals which are said to live there. They probably hide from all those people that stroll around in their tree tops. I guess if I were an animal, I would do the same. Anyway, the main idea seems to be the fun of walking around on this shaky construction. I am not afraid of height, so to me it isn't such a big deal, but to Stephen it was obviously an enormous challenge as he had told me beforehand. He wanted to hold my hand all the time, and sometimes it was a bit hard to move with all of his weight clinging on to me. Well, altogether it was fun and definitely worth going there. Stephen even saved some money by telling them that I was his wife. You know, they have here different prices for locals and for foreigners. They even do this in a very open way with lists hanging out that clearly indicate the two different prices.

Here in Ghana they find it totally normal that as a white person you have to pay considerably more. Just that as an African's wife you may be counted as an African pricewise, provided that your man does a convincing job in discussing with them. After all, nobody can be expected to carry their marriage licence along. ☺

We later chatted a bit with two American girls. Stephen, who is by now already used to playing tourist guide, equipped them with quite a few tips on what to do and where to go. He also pointed out to them as he had done to me before that they should be careful with the Nigerians. It seems that he really hates them. You know, he always tells me that I shouldn't open the door of my hotel room to anyone. He thinks this could be really dangerous.

When we walked along this crowded, busy street that leads to the hotel, he did something that really irritated me. You know, you can see all kinds of people squatting right next to the road. There was also some old man sitting there, and he had his leg a bit stretched out. The way it looked to me, his leg probably hurt, and there wasn't really much choice where to put it. I mean, Stephen and I definitely had enough space to pass by, yet all of a sudden Stephen aggressively kicked the leg of this shaky old man away. I was quite shocked. I would have never thought that he could do something like this. He just pointed out that those folks take up way too much space and that they are no good anyway.

He also claims that poor people purposely stick out their feet so that maybe a car will roll over, and then they will ask for some compensation money. Well, I know that everywhere in this world poor people have all kinds of tricks how to get by. But this was just an old man! Somebody way past working age. So you cannot even blame him for not getting a job or whatever. I really don't know what to think about it. The feeling I had was definitely not a nice one. All of a sudden I felt a lot of distance between me and Stephen. Yet I didn't dare to say anything. I just knew by instinct that I wouldn't get through to him.

When we arrived at the hotel, he got a phone call. The hospital needed a replacement for someone who had just fallen ill. They even offered to pay him a taxi.

As for me, I was happy to see him leave. I needed some time to be alone with my own thoughts.

For tomorrow he has made arrangements to show me his "dream house". He has already told me so much about it in his mails.

…
I probably should try to get sufficient sleep and gain some distance. Tomorrow is another day, hopefully!

Wish you all the best and thanks that you are always there for me.

Love,
Linda

6th of February, at 7 am

Hi Linda,

I can imagine that it must feel quite tense if all of a sudden you don't feel comfortable with the only person you know there.
Please be careful!

Until tonight,
Carla

6th of February, at 11 pm

Dear Carla,
Thanks for your concern. But please don't worry
about me. I shouldn't even have mentioned it!
Guess, I just overreacted.

Today we went a bit out of Accra to the rather
rural and rudimentary area where the "dream
house" is located. Stephen had borrowed a car,
and on the way there we stopped in some village
where Steve owns a room. It's something that we
would consider a store room because it has no
window. But since I could also spot a mattress
inside, someone is obviously sleeping there. Stephen went to speak with a prospective tenant,
and the other guy handed over some money. Stephen explained to me later that in Ghana you
always pay the rent for a full year in advance. By
the end of that period you either move out or you
prolong your arrangement. That way the owner
can always be sure to get his money.
And you have to know that electricity works here
similar to some of those mobile phones in Austria. You have a card on which you can book a
certain credit. And when your credit is used up,
you either have to get a new card or you will sit
in the dark until you are able to do so. But at
least, that way you cannot build up debts for
electricity bills.

211

The dream house is basically finished except for the door and the windows. It's got solid walls, a living room and two bedrooms. Stephen also showed me where the bath will be and pointed out that it is big enough to fit a bathtub. He also explained that traditionally you have the kitchen outside on the porch because they cook with firewood, and those ovens produce quite a bit of smoke.

He also explained to me that water is a problem in the area. Well, I'm used to problems with water supply from living in Spain, but Ghana is still a different problem-level, it seems. At times every household gets water only once a week, and you never know when the pipes in your neighbourhood will suddenly overflow. You better be home then or have a neighbour who will inform you, so that you can either run home quickly or make arrangements. Best to fill up every vessel you can get a hold of with water so that it will last you until next time. It's also an opportunity to have a shower and to do your laundry. And you can wash your bike or car; or even your dog. For us it's hard to imagine, but the people in Accra are used to it. Yet they know that this is not normal and that in other corners of the world, water is available at any time you open the tap.

On the other hand, it is a fact that in Ghana there are also amazingly rich people who show off their fleet of up to fifteen expensive cars and live in houses that look like castles. And the poor people seem to think that outside of Africa everybody lives like the extremely rich in Accra. And as much as I have pointed out to Stephen that the vast majority of people in Europe are not "rich" in the sense Africans define this word, I always have the feeling that he cannot truly believe this.

I expressed my congratulations concerning the building shell. We walked around and took some pictures of me leaning comfortably out of the window, like the lady of the house. He expressed some hope that maybe someday I could build my own house on his ground, in case I needed more privacy. I just smiled and avoided any direct answer. I said I would have to think about this for a longer time. But maybe sometime in the future when the children will be grown-up, I might consider it. That was enough to keep him happy for the moment. As for me, I don't know. Since things have taken such an unfortunate turn in Spain I'm actually looking for a new "paradise" somewhere in the world, and so far I haven't found it. But could it be Accra? Africa is in general a place with vast nature and few people, which is something I like. But Accra is a densely populated area and there are too many people and too much confusion for my taste. Again, out there where the dream house is located, you totally miss any kind of infrastructure. You definitely need your own transport vehicle there, or you are grounded. On one hand, I feel that the neighbouring houses are built much too close. There is not enough space left for any plants or sufficient distance between the buildings. On the other hand, I would be afraid to stay there alone when Stephen is at work. I never feel comfortable in small houses anyway because someone could get inside way too easily. I just wouldn't feel safe.

Later we went back to the city. We got stuck in traffic for two hours until we finally made it somewhere to a coastal area. There we sat down to chat some more, and we had a refreshment. I looked at the menu and thought at first that this must be a mistake, but Stephen confirmed that the price of the fish was really 90 dollars!!
I still find it hard to understand that restaurants and shops are adapted here only to the rich! Just like Accra Shopping Mall where you can probably buy anything you could possibly think of, but only if you are wealthy.
Talking about being rich then led to some conversation about voodoo. So far I had never taken voodoo seriously. To me this was only some kind of superstition. But I soon found out that to Stephen voodoo is something very real. He told me that there were people who could for example

214

put an evil spell on a chair and when a person sits down on it, he or she will get severely sick.

He also told me that there exists some kind of ritual that will make you rich. Just that you need the head of a child to perform this spell. I voiced some doubt that such a spell could work, but I could soon see that he believed in it a hundred percent. He claimed that there had been cases of children who had disappeared because of such practise. It kind of shocked me when he pointed out that as a faithful Christian he would never do something like this; but that it definitely worked and that there were quite a few people here in Accra who had gained their fortune that way. He told me that the corpses of those poor children sometimes turned up again somewhere in a gutter but with the head missing.

The part that shocked me was that around here you have to be a Christian so you will not consider doing something like that. I've come to understand certain statements in a different way by now. Normally this exaggerated confirmation that they are Christians, and this churchy attitude would just go on my nerves. But here it means that at least they will not consider killing children for rituals that could get them from rags to riches.

I guess there is nothing left to say. I've googled the topic tonight in the hotel room. I found only two articles that confirmed that there had been such cases of abducted children. Yet, those claims that they were used for witchcraft was considered a lie in order to discredit African people.

Oh well, I remember having heard similar stories in Kenya. There they think that albino children are very valuable for witchcraft and therefore those tend to be stolen from their parents.

It's a crazy place!!

Thanks for listening!
Bye, Linda

7th of February, at 7 am

Dear Linda,

I always told you that I consider Accra a town which I would never ever consider travelling to. I'm definitely worried about you because you are all alone in such a place. If anything went wrong with your Stephen, what would you do? Or maybe the question should be: What could you do?

It drives me crazy just to think about it. So I'm glad that in two days you will hopefully be on your way back.

Please be careful!
Carla

7th of February, at 11 pm

Dear Carla,

Please don't worry about me. Everything is fine.

Today we went to a beach since I pointed out that I would be disappointed if I couldn't even go swimming once during a stay in a town that is located by the ocean.

As Stephen pointed out before, it's not so easy since the places where the poor people go are not safe. So we went to a beach at the other end of town where the rich people go for a swim. Already the entrance was around ten dollars a person. And there is a life guard who probably cannot swim himself! I mean, this guy was fully dressed, and I wondered how he could save anyone in this outfit. But I guess he sees his job more in preventing people from going in too far. He went on my nerves because he continuously waved at me, indicating that I should come back out to where the water barely touched my knees. He made himself very important, blowing that stupid whistle. It got kind of ridiculous when he actually claimed that there was somewhere a deep hole where one could suddenly lose ground and drown. Well, since I noticed that Stephen felt quite nervous when I went out even a little bit further, I just lay down a bit in the flat water.

Interesting to mention, there was hardly any other person swimming there!!

I think Stephen was very relieved when we finally were sitting in the shade, having a drink. We talked about all kinds of things and decided to pass by some market in order to buy a few giant mangoes and other stuff for me to take back.

Yes, tomorrow evening my flight back is already scheduled! Unbelievable, how fast such a week can fly by!

We didn't stay too long at the beach, and I wasn't exactly sad to leave since it was a bit boring. I guess Stephen was there for the first time in his life, but now he even considers going there some time with his kids.

On the way out our feet were full of sand. A man with a bucket of water was already waiting there for clients, but I didn't want to spend money on this service. Only a few metres away I spotted the sink where he got his water from. So I just went there and washed off the sand in the basin.

Later, as we strolled along some market, we passed by a stand where they sold huge snails. It was new to me that also on land there exist snails that have practically the size of a small watermelon. Stephen explained to me that they are used for making soup. As I got ready to take some pictures of the snails, the lady who sold them started to freak out. So Stephen talked to her for quite a while, and in the end he managed to calm her down. He explained to me that this woman was highly worried about being photographed herself.

Well, in some places of this world people think that if you take their picture, they will lose their soul. I even personally know a man who was in his youth arrested in Morocco, for the theft of a soul! As we assured her that she wouldn't be in the picture she even allowed me to hold the creature whose body felt nice and cool on my hot skin. And due to the fact that I actually like snails, this animal definitely made my day.

We returned to the hotel, and Stephen ordered some local food which we ate in the room. Afterwards Stephen wanted to go to a restaurant where you can listen to African music. It turned out that it wasn't exactly easy to find such a place since they all unfortunately didn't have live music that evening. Stephen got a little irritated, and I got tired of walking around for so long. I told him that I didn't mind and that it wasn't worth wasting the last evening we had here together just running around. He finally agreed, and we went to sit down in a small restaurant by the beach. As the evening progressed some local musician came by to play a few songs. Stephen didn't like his performance and also told him so.

219

I felt kind of sorry for the guy and pointed out to Steve that it wasn't so easy to sing and play just with a cheap guitar without any microphone or amplifying equipment.

I was a bit worried about the people on a table next to us since one could tell that they were smoking marihuana. I didn't want the smell to catch in my clothes and hair. After all, the dogs at the airport might still be able to pick out the smell, even one day later. Those dogs are well trained, and their nose is so much better than ours! So, if even I can notice that smell in my jacket there is reason to be worried, I guess. I mean, my hair I can still wash, but the jacket wouldn't get dry anymore.

We didn't stay too long.

Tomorrow Stephen will bring me to the airport already in the early afternoon, just to make sure that I'll be there before the heavy traffic will block the streets again.

Tomorrow morning I plan to write one last time from Accra. Later I will be on my way and unable to access the internet till I'm back home. I will also drop you a line as soon as I have safely arrived in my flat in Vienna.

Then you can finally stop worrying about me! ☺

Thanks for everything.

Hugs,
Linda

8th of February, at 7 pm

Dear Linda,

That's a good idea that you are still going to write to me before you go and then again after your arrival back home.

Have a safe trip!
Hugs
Carla

8th of February, at 11 pm

Dear Carla,

You cannot imagine how ready I am to go home! The last night was absolutely horrible.
At some time around 2 am somebody knocked at my door. I mean, actually he pounded against it and started screaming. I think he thought that this was his room because he also tried to open with a key. Since the door didn't move, he started kicking it with his feet, and I was afraid that he might succeed in breaking it open. I yelled something just to let him know that the room was already occupied, and he screamed back that I should open the door. He sounded quite aggressive and

of course, I didn't open. I called the reception and tried to make myself understood to this young girl (the one who always woke me up in the morning to announce that breakfast was ready). She promised to get someone to check and told me not to open, no matter what. In the meantime the man had left, and I thought that he had probably realised that this was not his room. It took me a while until I could calm down, but just as I was about to fall asleep there was noise again out in the hall. I could hear footsteps of several people, but I couldn't understand their words. They definitely sounded unfriendly and dangerous. A woman screamed hysterically, and a man yelled at her. I could hear a noise that sounded like he had just slapped her, and then she screamed again. Then they left, but after a few minutes suddenly something pounded against my door with a big bang, and next someone tried again to enter my room. By what he said, this guy was convinced that inside of my room there was his wife because he kept ordering me to open, screaming and swearing in English, accusing me of all kinds of things that I had supposedly done to him. His voice sounded drunken and aggressive, and I have to admit that at that point I felt really afraid. It took a long time until it was silent again, and after that I was way too alarmed to find any sleep. Sometime later the girl from the reception called and said that the security guard of the hotel had passed by my room but hadn't seen anybody. I told her that it was finally quiet, and she told me to phone again in case there were any further problems.

After some sleepless hours I finally made myself some tea and ate the bananas which were the only food left. I hadn't tried them at all since they were freckled with dark spots, already on the day of my arrival. Normally I don't like over-ripe bananas, but in the middle of this crazy night, I figured, I might as well eat them anyway. I tried one of them, and it was a pleasant surprise. It had a flowery smell and an amazingly rich and aromatic flavour. So in the end I ate up the whole bundle.

In the morning I took a bath and started to pack everything together. It was hard to fit the mangoes, and I just hope they won't turn into juice.

When Stephen came, I told him about the turbulent night I had had. He blamed it again on "the Nigerians" without having seen the people. I didn't understand how he could be so sure about that, but it didn't matter anymore.

My focus was already on leaving anyway. And this incident increased my readiness to go home.

Well, I really have to say that I am very thankful that all of this happened in the last night and not in the first one. Because, if it had happened in the beginning, I would have never been able to feel at ease in this room, not even for a minute.

Whatever, thanks for everything. It was definitely reassuring for me to know that you were there for me in the background, ready to help, if anything really had gone wrong.

Right now I have to get ready to meet Stephen. We still have to pick up my valuables, including the emergency money, from the reception safe. And I still want to buy a few spices for Clarissa at the market area around the corner.
You will hear from me next when I am at home.
Yours,
Linda

9th of February, at 11pm

Dear Carla,

I have arrived home safely after a tiring flight.
Thanks again. Unfortunately something has come up here during my absence. But you know how it is. If you have a family, there is always some domestic drama lurking in the background. I'll tell you about it when we see each other next time in person.

Hugs
Linda

10th of February 2012
Dear Stephen,

Sorry that I didn't write immediately after coming home, but things in my place were not quite the way I would have imagined it.

Well, it's a bit hard for me to get started …

As soon as I had opened the door with my key, my "normal life" took a grip on me again. I hadn't even taken off my winter jacket yet when Kate walked up to me and started crying heavily. She just sobbed that something horrible had happened. I immediately suspected that she had probably lost her job. You know, around here, if you are sick for too long a time, you get easily fired. I mean, they are not allowed to fire you because you are sick, but they always find some accepted reason to do so. Well, I put my arm around her and was just about to say that this wouldn't be the end of the world when suddenly I was hit by the information that Kate's father had died. Wow, that sure was a totally unexpected surprise! I tried to be compassionate even though it was a bit strange to see her so emotionally involved, crying about the loss of a father whom she had never known and who had never cared about her. About a man who had tried to force me to have an abortion. When he didn't succeed, he ended the relationship at first. Yet some weeks later he suddenly called again. You know, at that point he acted like he had now come to accept the situation. So we dated again, and after a very nice evening I stayed overnight in his place. Then, while I was sleeping, he suddenly attacked me, with the intention to get the baby out of my body by force. I ended up in hospital that night, and he was questioned by the police. Shortly before Kate's birth he wanted contact again. He said that he was sorry and that he was now ready to take up his responsibility as a father. But I suspect this was just good advice from his lawyer. After all, there was still a trial ahead! You know, you can't avoid that here because the hospital notifies the police, and the police have to prosecute any criminal assault. Interestingly enough, exactly a few weeks after the trial, he vanished again without a word of explanation. The only good thing was that exactly at that time when he disappeared, I had anyway come to the conclusion that I wanted to end this relationship …

As I was looking at poor Kate, I kind of marvelled about the fact that she could feel so much grief. But I understand it to a certain point. I think she is just sad about the fact that she will never have the chance to meet him. That there won't be a possibility to work out their nonexistent relationship. Death is always so final. It puts a definite end to all those secret hopes and illusions we might have …

Next Clarissa came around the corner and told me that there had been a problem with the heating system which is, of course, very unfortunate with low winter temperatures outside. Too bad! Actually I had specifically tried to avoid such a situation by ordering a plumber for inspection shortly before I left. But I guess this handyman wasn't a good one.

Lori seems to feel extremely sorry for Kate because she hops around her like a private nurse. In the meantime Kate's injuries are healing and soon she will have to go back to work.

Well, Stephen, I'm sorry that I have no better news to tell. But you know how life can be at times.

I still want to thank you for the time in Accra. It was a very interesting experience for me, and I will never forget it.

Love,
Linda

12th of February 2012

Dear Linda,

Oh my god! What a shock it must have been for you! I can understand your feelings, and I wish I could be there to comfort you.

By the way, I hadn't realised that Kate had a different father. I don't think you ever mentioned it.

I still wish to express that it was very special to me to have you here at least for a week. I hope you can understand better now how we live here in Accra. And I have to admit that I miss you already now. I kind of got used to picking you up every day. It's too bad we cannot go on like this. But the next time you come, I hope the dream house will already be in such a condition that you can comfortably stay there. Then you don't have to stay in a hotel with all kinds of weird people around.

I've just looked at the photographs I have taken and I really like most of them. They will remind me forever of the time we shared together.

By the way, the children really liked their presents, and they have eaten up all the sweets by now. Penny also loved her treat, and she gulped it down very quickly. Thank you again for everything.

Hugs and kisses.

Yours always, Steve

14th of February 2012
Dear Stephen,

Thanks for your kind words.
It always feels strange returning to Vienna after having been away to a place that is so completely different; a place where you have no set identity, no obligations, and no past experiences to deal with. You suddenly have this wonderful distance to your own life. But as soon as you go back, your normal environment comes down on you, and this can feel very strenuous. I don't know if you can imagine that …
I haven't even had time yet to look at the photographs I took, but I'm sure that there will also be quite a few nice ones. As soon as I can manage, I will send you the best ones. It will anyway take some time because more than three pictures don't fit into a mail, due to data limits for attachments. But I think it doesn't matter if it takes a bit longer. Could be a bit like those advent calendars which we have in Austria where you can open a new window every day in the last twenty-four days before Christmas. Nowadays there are usually some sweets behind those windows, but in the past there was only every day a new picture ☺
Well, Stephen, I wish you all the best and a good day at work!
Love, Linda

15th of February 2012
Dear Linda,

How are you, and how are your children? How is Kate doing? It must be an extremely challenging time for her.

Thanks for wishing me a good time at work. Some people there have known about your visit, and they are quite nosy, asking all kinds of questions which I, of course, rarely answer! You remember that one day when we stopped with the car outside the hospital because I had to pick up something there? You know, some of my colleagues looked outside and saw you sitting in the car, and of course they immediately asked a lot of questions. They are nice people, and knowing that I am divorced, I guess most of them are really happy for me. But sometimes it's a bit too much.

Anyway, please don't strain yourself too much, and don' forget to eat and sleep enough.

Hugs,
Stephen

16th of February 2012
Dear Stephen,

I am ok, so don't worry about me.

I've spoken today with Kate's half-sister, and she gave me some details concerning the death of her father. It seems that he has been sick already for a longer time with lung cancer. I recall that he was a heavy smoker, and actually just being together with him for about seven months has caused me a permanent lung problem. Ever since I have been coughing heavily every morning, and it is kind of hard for me to catch my breath. Sounds weird that this extreme sensitivity of the lungs stayed with me, even after this man was long gone! Sure, as my doctor pointed out, there is probably a hereditary component to it, too. And a chain smoking mother probably wasn't good for me either. But you know, when I was a kid there existed practically no awareness at all about the fact that smoking is dangerous to people's health. It was considered cool and modern for a woman to smoke then.

Whatever, knowing about his lifestyle, my sympathy is limited. I guess it's fair that *he* died of his cigarettes and not *I*. But still I have to live with this damage he has done to my life. Physically as well as psychologically. You know, since this incident when he tried to get the baby out of my body while I was sleeping, I could never again sleep comfortably in the presence of a man. I just feel so alarmed that I cannot fall asleep.

So I can say that this relationship has had a permanent effect on me but not a good one. Of course, it is always somewhat touching if a person you have been close to suddenly dies, and I guess I've sounded a bit emotional at certain points of my conversation with that half-sister. So she actually invited me to the funeral! But I think this would really be too much.

Kate has asked her sister Alicia to accompany her to the funeral, and that will be fine.

I have to leave now.

Hugs,
Linda

17th of February 2012
Dear Linda,

I can imagine that this situation is extremely burdening for you. All those unfortunate memories being stirred up again! When will the funeral take place? I hope afterwards the situation will calm down and you all will find some peace of mind. I pray that the Lord will heal your heart.

Take good care of yourself, my love!

Yours always
Stephen

20th of February 2012
Dear Stephen,

The funeral finally took place yesterday. I'm glad I wasn't there because from what I've heard all the people present were heavy smokers. I mean how grotesque can it be. A man just died long before his due time because he had lung cancer from smoking and then you crowd together smoking at his funeral. Well, it's obviously an addiction. Nobody could seriously choose for that out of a free mind. But I guess in some ways people get what they have asked for …
At least Kate's half-sister and Kate don't smoke, so maybe there is at least some hope for their future, health-wise. Just that this sister has a husband who smokes, and all her relatives do. So she has to put up with a lot of passive smoking just like me in the past.

Seems that this is something Kate has understood in the course of time: That smoking is not cool!! Because I remember times when she was little when she even snatched cigarettes out of some construction worker's jacket. I don't recall who caught her in the end, but it was a bigger deal, and the lady from the day-care place reported it to me in a rather agitated way. Of course, one could have led the discussion in different ways. For example, by asking how little Kate had even been able to get a hold of those cigarettes. After all, you should probably not let dangerous substances lying around right next to a playground. And why didn't the childcare worker notice? After all, she gets paid for watching the children. Anyway, I had a longer talk with Kate about the issue, pointing out how stupid it is to smoke, what a waste of money and what a danger to a person's health. I guess it impressed her when I said that a heavy smoker could well have the value of a house going up in smoke in the course of a lifetime. And she even remembered years later my remark that people with a cigarette in their mouth look to me like a baby that is frantically sucking its pacifier. Nothing cool about it.

Whatever, the nice thing to report is that the half-sister did a good job at somehow including Kate at the funeral. She even had both their names written on the banner that accompanied the floral tribute.

Well, you have to know that this young woman had always wished for a sibling. Yet, when they first got in contact, she already had a baby herself, and Kate was already about ten years old …

I hope emotions will calm down again eventually.

Hope things are fine in your place.
Yours,
Linda

21st of February 2012
My dearest Linda,

It's good to hear that it's all over. Time will take care of it, believe me!
Say, how did Kate and her half-sister ever get to know each other?

Sorry, that I don't have time to write more today. I'm already under high pressure to make it to work. But I didn't want to leave without dropping you at least a few lines, my dear.
So, be assured of my love always,
Stephen

22nd of February 2012
Hi Stephen,

Thanks for still saving a minute for me despite of already being in a hurry.
That sure is sweet of you!

Well, concerning Kate and her half-sister, it seems that she kept telling both her parents that she wished for a sister. Her parents were divorced, and she probably felt lonely at times. Anyway, at some point her father told her that she actually had a little sister from his side. But he admitted that there was no contact.
Years later she investigated our address and some day she just rang at our door. My husband opened, and she explained herself. Well, my husband informed her that actually Kate and I weren't living there anymore, but he gave her my phone number. And then eventually there came this initial phone call when she finally reached me. Now I have to say that I have a big heart when it comes to such stories. I would never be in the way of a young girl wishing to meet her half-sister. She reminded me so much of myself when I tried to find my father and someday rang at his door. I know from experience how much courage you have to pick up in order to do so. And I know how much it hurts if, like in my

case, you have to find out that you are not welcome.

So I really tried my best to go along with her wishes. We initially arranged to meet in her place; and from that time she called me on a regular basis to stay updated about Kate. She also started to send her Christmas- and birthday presents. When Kate was a bit older, they had direct contact, and she was sometimes even invited to her sister's new home in the countryside.

Have a wonderful day at work and enjoy the warm weather because here it is freezing cold right now.

Love,
Linda

23rd of February 2012
My dearest Linda,

What an interesting story!
I find it very generous that you agreed to let them have contact after all the evil this man has done to you. But you are probably right because the things her father has done are not this girl's fault
…

237

By the way, I just ordered some windows and a door for the dream house. It might take a while until they arrive. But I'm getting really excited about it!!

You will see, next time you come, the house will be ready to use!!

Hugs and kisses
Stephen

28th of February 2012
Dear Stephen,

Wow, that's really exciting! Looks like the dream house will be ready for you sooner than you thought! What a wonderful development! I still remember times when you had some doubt if you would ever be able to finish it at all!

On the 1st of April I'm going to Tenerife with Kate and Lori. I hope they will like it there. Actually I had planned to go there already during Christmas vacation but as you know, Kate started this apprenticeship in fall, and when I signed the contract, I forgot to mention that we had already booked a holiday. So, due to this mistake, the manager later on made a big statement out of it. You know, all about how rules will be rules and have to be kept by everyone. And according to the law, if you have just started working for a company you have no right to holidays during the first six months. Well, it's ridiculous, but because I forgot to ask before signing, we all had to cancel that holiday! We booked a new one for the Easter holidays at least.

Now the manager is probably grumpy again because Kate has already been away from work for so long. You have to imagine, the other day she called me to ask how much longer this sick leave still would last. I told her that it was the doctor's job to give clearance for work, but she kind of acted like Kate was making herself a nice, comfortable time at home while everybody else had to do her work. She also asked me about how this accident had happened, and she started to lecture me about the candle. How I could possibly allow candles in the house! She pointed out that by law all candles had to have some glass protection around them and how they at work had only such ones. It made me kind of furious because that law might apply to restaurants, but such a traditional Advent wreath that is sold here at markets or shops never has glass around the candles. The wreath is made from brushwood, and the candles are stuck on in a rather simple way, either with liquid wax or with the help of some metal wire. Now, should we sue the shop where Lori bought this object?! Besides, it's ridiculous because above the flame the glass protection is open, and this accident happened when Kate reached over the flame, so her shirt would have caught fire anyway. You know, she was just talking smart, trying to blame it somehow on me. I mean, I had told Kate that this candle looked dangerous to me, the way she handled it. What can I do if next day she just lights it again? I don't know every move that is going on in this room of hers. After all, in her age you have a right to some privacy. This girl is sixteen and I don't have to supervise her at all, apart from giving proper info and advice. And this I did.

I think it wasn't about facts. This manager probably regrets the bonus they paid Kate shortly before the accident. Because this you get only if your work is top-class and you haven't missed a day. I remember the first info before Kate even started was: You better don't get sick during the three-month probation period. Because if you do, you will be fired immediately.

On one hand I understand that the people who work on this intermediate management level have a lot of stress because they get pressure from up and down. But I don't like it. I don't like this heartless business world. It's all about how much profit they can make on you. And how to enhance this gain by keeping their worker's share as little as possible. Just thinking about it makes me feel highly irritated.

Sorry for being so negative today. I didn't intend to stretch this out in such an extended mail. Guess I was just pretty upset.

Thanks for listening to all of this.

Love,
Linda

2nd of March 2012
My beloved Linda,

Will you please never again excuse yourself for telling me about whatever happens to be on your heart! I feel honoured that I am the person you talk to. And you know, life being what it is, there will always be days when we are burdened with problems of whatever kind.
I find the behaviour of this manager absolutely outrageous. I mean, you have saved your daughter's life! And now somebody even accuses you that this accident could have been your fault?! How crazy life can be!

Thanks for your kind and assuring words concerning the dream house. I hope you can stay there next time you come.

By the way, what have you planned to do in Tenerife with the kids?

Here in my place there is nothing new.
Hugs,
Stephen

5th of March 2012
Dear Stephen,

It's great to have a friend like you who is always there for me and who is always on my side. I really appreciate your loyalty.

As for going on holiday with the kids, I want to visit the famous Loro Park for sure. And I would like to find a place where you can go swimming with dolphins. Kate is really fond of those animals, and I remember doing such programmes in the Dominican Republic and in Cuba. Now, it's a fact that I cannot take Kate to such a country because she suffers from severe motion sickness. But maybe in Tenerife something will come up.

Be happy if there is nothing new in your place. As you know, no news is good news! ☺
Yours always,
Linda

7th of March 2012
My dearest Linda,

I'm sure that it will be an experience for the children to have close contact with a dolphin. Those animals are even used for therapy, and after almost dying in a fire, this might have a healing effect on your daughter's psychological condition.

As for me I have travel plans to go to the north of Ghana. I think I have mentioned this to you a longer time ago …
There is a region with a lake where they have half-wild crocodiles. I will send you a link where you see people who actually take pictures with them. They are tame enough that you can even pet them and kiss them on the snout!! It's been one of the true wishes of my heart to go there for a long time, and someday I will. Maybe already next year. But right now I need whatever money is left over for the dream house, as you know.

Have a wonderful day.
Stephen

9th of March 2012
Dear Stephen,

Oh, that video is quite amazing. I can understand that you want to go there!
And if it takes a while before you can go, you can enjoy the anticipation even longer. ☺
As you know, I myself like booking trips long beforehand because this gives me something pleasant to live up to. ☺
The dream house of course comes first. This is a lasting value which you will enjoy for the rest of your life.
Holidays are nice to have, but way too soon they change into mere remembrance …
(Yet on the other hand, it's also valuable to create beautiful memories … ☺)

Thanks for your kind words concerning Kate.
Best wishes for your day!
Linda

11th of March 2012
Dear Linda,

You always encourage me so much, my dear! Of course I would love it best if we could go to this crocodile lake together! I walked past Kwame

Nkrumah Circle yesterday and as I visited the night market, I noticed how much I miss you already again. I went to the place where we sat down with our snack and where we have been talking for a long time. I, with my arm around your shoulder, and you, with your head resting comfortably against my chest. Too bad that I cannot beam you here at times!
Take care of yourself!
I need you so much!
Stephen

14th of March 2012
Dear Stephen,

Today Kate had to start working again. She phoned me up crying before she even went there. Knowing what it is like at work, she obviously didn't feel capable of going there. I promised to phone the manager, to inform her that she couldn't expect full performance yet. She was kind of nice and understanding about it and promised not to overwork her. I think it was ok then. From what she told at home, all the colleagues were very nice and helpful whenever there was need to lift something heavy. So hopefully things will fall in place again.
Love, Linda

16th of March 2012
Dear Linda,

Today I want to share with you a weird story. I
don't quite know what to think about it. I have an
online pal from India who has been writing to me
for quite some time. She is still very young, I
think eighteen, and still living with her family.
Her father is very protective and often locks her
in because it is not safe in their neighbourhood.
Her mother died when she was only ten, and the
dad quickly found himself a new wife, a widow
with a little boy who is by now fourteen years
old. So, recently the father has ordered this stepbrother to take care of the girl to the point that he
even sleeps in the same room, like her personal
body guard. Now she has written to me that she
seems to be pregnant, and she doesn't quite understand how this could have happened. She
cannot remember having had sex with anyone,
just that one night she woke up, and this brother
was lying in bed next to her. So, knowing that I
work in a hospital, she has asked me how this
could be possible. Well, I asked her a few questions, and it seems she remembers a discharge
from her vagina that day. So it looks like that
boy had sex with her while she was sleeping, and
she hasn't even noticed it! What a crazy story!
Do you think that this is possible? I mean that
she has really not noticed anything at all at the

moment when the act took place? It's a little bit hard to imagine, but she seems to be honest in her statements, and I guess she wasn't even informed properly about the facts of life. It's hard to imagine, and this situation will be a disaster once her father finds out about it. I mean, he was so careful, but they have underestimated this little brother. Guess they assumed that he was still a child, but you cannot trust a boy of this age. Even if they have grown up as siblings. At least it is not incest after all because they are not related by blood.

I will be interested to hear your opinion.

Take care, my love
Stephen

20th of March 2012
Dear Stephen,

I have a hard time imagining that all of this really happened without the girl noticing anything at all. Ok, I understand that she doesn't know what sex is all about, and it happened while she was sleeping. Maybe she was in some kind of state between waking and dreaming. Maybe she thought she was dreaming and forgot the whole action again, just like we often forget dreams as soon as we wake up. I could imagine that due to inhibition she might have blocked out this experience to the point of not knowing about it anymore.

Of course, it would also make a lot of sense if she just chose not to know anything about it. It's kind of a naive way out of the problem that leaves her without guilt. Because, if she doesn't know that something happened, how can it then be her fault? Whatever, if the girl is pregnant now, something must have happened. But I've heard of cases where girls conceived even without actual penetration. I recall reading some weird article a long time ago where doctors did some research on the topic and in the end confirmed that in some rare cases it seems to be possible that sperms creep in from the outside and still make it all the way up. One way or the other, the poor girl will have to deal with the consequences now. Too bad! I really feel sorry for her.

Hope you have a pleasant day at work

Linda

22nd of March 2012

My dear Linda,

I didn't know that there exist even studies concerning the topic.

In the meantime this girl is of course very afraid of her father. She thinks he might even kill her in case the news should hit him in the wrong moment. I have told her that she has to talk to someone about it because the longer she waits, the bigger the problem will be in the end. Unless she should have a natural miscarriage, the problem will definitely not take care of itself.

How is your daughter doing at work? It must be hard for her.

By the way, how are Lori and Cora? We haven't spoken about them for a longer time, have we!

Hope to hear from you soon.

Yours,
Stephen

26th of March 2012
Dear Stephen,

It's good that this Indian girl has at least an online friend like you who can give her some reasonable advice. You are right, she has to talk to someone and the family has to think about the best possible solution. Not that this will be easy. But something needs to be done and arranged. The sooner the better!

Kate still has a hard time tackling the challenges of work. At first, everybody was very understanding, but in the meantime they expect her more and more to perform as she did before the accident. But this is not possible. And it just seems that nobody understands that. It will possibly take her a long time to get back to the level of her former condition. If she ever will!

Lori has turned fourteen in the meantime and she is having a good time at school. Her marks are top and she is very successful concerning the music-focus of this class. I think you know that in her school everybody has to learn an instrument, and they also have a band and a choir. Regular music performances in public are part of the programme, and that way they are continuously preparing for some concert. Just two days ago I was in school for a parents' evening, and what her music teacher told me was almost too good to believe. He stated that in his opinion Lori wasn't only the best in her piano group. No, she can also play the guitar better than the guitarists of the school. And she can sing better than the singers! I know that he has always considered her extremely talented. This was the reason why he had taken her into the school band already in second grade even though participation in this band is normally reserved for the third and fourth grade. Now in the past, this obvious preferential treatment of Lori was at times a source of great trouble. There was a girl one grade ahead of her who was the best of her class. She was somehow extremely jealous of Lori, who, at that time, just couldn't handle the situation at all. Lori was crying about how that girl was kind of mobbing her, and upset to the point that she didn't want to go to those band rehearsals anymore. The music teacher kept a distance to those "personal problems" of his students. I understand that he is no psychologist, but still, I think he has a responsibility for whatever happens in his class room or his band, and I also told him so. I also don't like it that he smokes next to the children when he sometimes takes them for practise or recordings to his private home.

Anyway, this year that specific girl has already left school, so Lori can enjoy the music part without any nervy competition problems. I'm

251

very glad that her life develops so fine right now. The way it looks, she will be able to continue her education in another school that leads up to a so-called "Matura Diploma". It's not so easy to pass but enables you to study at any college or university you choose. (I think I've mentioned this diploma before)

So, at least Lori has a lucky strike right now. She really deserves it. I remember times in the past when she was still in elementary school ... She had this silly teacher then who didn't like her. I think this teacher played a great part in those frequent headaches, tommy aches and other states of indisposition which she permanently had at that time. You know, she really suffers from migraine, but such a teacher definitely makes things worse. So, I truly value the nice and productive atmosphere this school presents.

Little Cora is her usual sweet self as always!

Hugs,
Linda

27th of March 2012
Hi Linda,

It was nice to hear about Lori and her success at school. She seems to be quite a talent.
I realise that your holiday is coming up already in four days, so I guess that you will already be quite busy.
Wish I could come along with you guys!
Hahaha!!!
But one is allowed to have dreams, isn't one? ☺

Please, write before you go! I will miss hearing from you for a full week!

Hugs and kisses,
Stephen

30th of March, 2012
Dear Stephen,

Just a few quick lines to say good-bye for the next week.
I haven't finished packing yet and at the same time there are still quite a few lessons scheduled, even more than usual! Many students still want to have an extra lesson this week due to the fact that I won't be available all of next week. The

same is true for the first days after my return. Also those days are practically overbooked. Good for my finances, but maybe not so good for the recreational impact which you also expect from taking a holiday. But well, let's not complain about something like this. ☺
I will write immediately after my return.
I wish you a pleasant week.
Love,
Linda

31st of March 2012
My beloved Linda,

I don't know if this mail will still reach you before you leave, but I still felt like writing it anyway. I wish you a great vacation and lots of fun with your children.
Take good care of yourself, and have a safe trip.
Yours always,
Stephen

8th of April 2012
Hi Stephen,

As you can see I am back again. ☺

Well, it was nice but in certain aspects a bit strange. The hotel was at some distance from the beach and basically ok. Just already in need for a few repairs. When we came in and opened the door of the wardrobe, it practically fell out! And when I plugged in the water cooker, this immediately produced a short circuit!

And just imagine, when we arrived late at night, they only handed us the keys and told us the corresponding floor. Just that they have a weird system of numbering all the doors; on the right side of the elevator with odd and on the left side with even numbers! Strange system! And if you are already tired from travelling, it can take a while until you check it out. I mean, they could mention it at check-in then it would all be clear!

Anyway, if you phone the reception, they at least come and repair things, but there was often a reason to phone them. Sometimes several times within one hour!

Whatever, what bothered me more, was the attitude of the people who worked there. I used to complain about the hotel staff in Cuba because the service was lousy, and they were only interested in our money. Every move they made and every smile cost extra!

Well, here in Tenerife our waiters practically surpassed them. They were even too lazy to fish for tips, and they didn't have a single smile to spare. They just moved around the dining hall like robots, totally ignoring the guests. I've never in my life seen anything like that!

The trip to Loro Park involved a long bus ride, and by the time we arrived, there was a huge crowd waiting at the entrance. When we finally were in, the kids didn't want to stay together, so one walked ahead, and the other stayed behind. It made me nervous because in this crowd you lose each other very easily. At some point Kate walked off angrily on purpose, so most of the time I was together with Lori. We went to see the dolphins and the orcas and of course the parrots and many more animals. The orcas really looked a bit too huge for their pool!

Well, I couldn't really enjoy most of the visit because I was so worried that Kate wouldn't make it back to the bus at the appointed time. And this was a scheduled bus that wouldn't be able to wait. And I really had no idea what to do, in case this situation might come up. Maybe I sometimes worry too much, but I already know by experience what all can go wrong. Besides, what should Kate do there all alone if she missed the bus? She doesn't speak Spanish and probably wouldn't know the name of the town where our hotel was located. And there were no later buses! So in case we waited for her until the park was empty and closed, how should we get home? A taxi might be expensive if you have to ride it for several hours!

Well anyway, we eventually found Kate again and enjoyed the rest of the time together.

One day we went to a place called Siam Park. It's a huge water fun park with many outstanding slides. There was one called "The Tower of Power" where you practically fall down straight, and you land in a pool where you can see sharks coming up to you. Luckily there is a glass wall between you and the sharks. ☺

There were other slides with coloured smoke inside, imitating a volcano, and some had all kinds of light effects and sounds. I would never get the idea to go to a place like this, but the kids liked it a lot. That's the interesting part about travelling with others; you might end up doing things that you would have never done on your own.

I'm glad that I found a place where they offer those dolphin programmes where you can actually get close to them. They don't advertise on large scale because there is a lobby of activists who consider those programmes to be "torture". But after asking around a bit, I got a promising hint. As we arrived there, we intended to book a programme called "swimming with dolphins" but were informed that it might probably be cancelled that day. I was a bit insistent to find out why, and eventually it turned out that they had the birth of a dolphin going on that day. Therefore it was their priority not to disturb the animals. Good for us, in the end it was possible to do at least a reduced programme. So one could pet a dolphin and get pictures taken. The trainer also taught us certain commands which they use to direct them. We also learned that there is even a whole set of commands used on international level. This makes it, of course, much easier to communicate with those animals.

Kate was touched when she noticed that the dolphin had a big scar on the belly which looked very similar to her own. We asked, and the girl told us that this dolphin had been attacked by a shark in Cuba. Environmentalists had saved its life and it was later brought to Tenerife because the local dolphinariums had no space.

Later we watched a very nice dolphin show. I liked it that they were very relaxed about it when some tricks didn't work. Kate was a bit sad, though, that she didn't get picked for actively taking part in the programme. But you know, going by the face she puts on, you could never guess how much she would love to participate.

But well, altogether it was a nice experience.

I don't think that I would like to visit Tenerife again. Mostly because of the people. I can well imagine that the local residents suffer a lot from too much tourism. Too many foreign influences that have invaded their island. That's why they kind of try to ignore them. On the other hand, they live off tourists, so it's an unsolvable dilemma.

Wow, this was quite a long mail!!
I hope everything is fine in your place.
Hugs,
Linda

9th of April 2012
Welcome back, Linda!

It sure was good to hear from you, after having spent a whole week without your mails. Thanks for telling me in detail about your trip. I'm glad Kate liked the dolphins. Yeah, in this age they are often a bit shy, or they try to look cool and if you don't know them, you could easily misinterpret their facial expressions.
Here there is nothing new. Lots of work, though, which is good for the realisation of the dream house. I often have to go there now in my free time to supervise the progress. But it's my pleasure to do so.
Love,
Stephen

11th of April 2012
Dear Stephen,

Yesterday was my late mother's birthday. It's such a day when I always think about how much of her life she has lost. I think she would have enjoyed seeing the children grow up.
You know, people always assure you that time heals all wounds. But I'm not any certain about this. Most of my life, my mother wasn't really present. But in recent years I somehow notice that the longer she's been gone for good, the more I miss her.

Say, by the way, what has happened to your Indian pal in the meantime?

Take good care of yourself.
Yours,
Linda

12th of April 2012
Hi Linda,

I'm sorry to hear about your mother.
You are so right! Some grief just stays with us forever! But I believe your mother is watching you from a distance. You know, dead people

often stay close to their loved ones for a long time. They can even help us.

When I was little, I used to weave baskets which we sold in town. One day, on the way home, I had an encounter with a spirit.

I was a bit afraid that day because the night had already fallen, and it was not so easy to find my path. All of a sudden there was this man who went ahead of me and called me to follow. He appeared to be kind of light in the darkness, and so I could easily find my way through the gloomy woods. I was very relieved when after a long walk I could finally see my house! I still wanted to say good-bye to the stranger. But suddenly he was gone again!

Later my grandmother told me that, according to my description of the man, she was sure that it was my deceased grandfather who had appeared to help me!

About the pal from India, I cannot report any good news. In the meantime her father is informed and he refuses an abortion because of religious beliefs. Looks like they will force her now to marry her stepbrother. She doesn't want this, though, and thinks of running away. But where can she go? What can she do somewhere else, especially if she is pregnant and later with a small baby along. If such a girl runs away from her village, the only means of survival will be

261

prostitution. I feel sorry for her but there is nothing I can do apart from writing a few compassionate and understanding words. I'm poor myself, and I am far away. I wish I could help her,
but there is unfortunately nothing I can do. It's
kind of depressing to think about it. Such a nice,
sweet, young girl, and already now her life is
ruined.

Linda, I miss you so much. I just wish you were
here, and we could take a walk by the beach and
share some banana chips or ice-cream.
Too bad that this is not possible right now. So,
for the moment I can only think of you and kiss
you in my dream.

Love
Steve

15th of April 2012
Dear Steve,

Sad to hear about your friend. But there is probably really nothing you can do.

About my mother: I normally feel the presence
of people who have passed away at times. But
my mother is gone and not within my reach an-

ymore. There have been occasions when I was very desperate and tried to contact her, but I couldn't. It would be nice to have this feeling that she is still somehow with me, but this is not the case. Yet, concerning the grandmother from my father's side, it's completely different. For a long time I could feel her presence, I could even see her, and she seemed to be watching me constantly. As if her own possibilities to find peace of mind, were somehow connected to me and my fate. As if I could break the vicious circle she had been caught in all her life. Don't ask me how I know this. I couldn't explain. I just know it. I'm sure you understand. Some things are almost impossible to explain; but if you happen to experience them, you need no explanation.

Love,
Linda

16th of April 2012
Dear Linda,

Of course, I understand. I'm sorry that you cannot experience this kind of bond with your mother.

I had a lot of trouble with my daughter today. She has some new computer game that she is very fond of right now. As I called her, she just ignored me. So I went to her room and ordered her to come, as I had a few things to tell her. And guess what? She just told me that I should wait because she wanted to finish her game first. This really upset me! I found it outrageous and disrespectful. I definitely cannot tolerate such behaviour in my house! So, as much as this might hurt me deep inside, I just had to discipline her. She screamed a lot during the beating because she is not used to such harsh treatment. But it is important to consequently stop such tendencies as soon as you can see them!

Hope things are fine in your place.
Yours,
Stephen

17th of April 2012
Hi Stephen,

What do you mean by "I had to discipline her"? If you choose to beat your daughter, it is not something you *have* to do. It's something you have decided for. So, don't act like it's an obligation!

Actually I think that your daughter's behaviour is quite normal for a teenaged girl. And if she is focused on her game and wants to finish it before she comes to you – is this really such a big problem? I mean, if it bothers you, can't you just talk to her about it? Or can't you be a bit more tolerant? I really consider this a minor issue. And I don't understand that you could actually beat her just because of something like this.

Linda

18th of April 2012

Hi Linda,

You see this completely wrong from your molly-coddled European point of view. In my country, the respect of a child for a parent means a lot, and I think it's one of our traditional values that we can be proud of. And as a father it is your responsibility to raise your kids in such a way that they will be valuable individuals. This is essential for our society as a whole. During puberty youngsters try to overthrow our rules, and at that point, we have to be careful. If we don't stop this behaviour immediately, it will soon be too late. Because such a child can easily turn into a rebellious and disrespectful young adult! This has to be avoided by all means!

I hope you understand.
Yours,
Stephen

19th of April 2012
Hi Stephen,

No, I don't understand. You act like you have to do this. But as I pointed out before, it is really your choice. You cannot always hide behind your society and your traditions. Also in my country it was normal to beat children if they didn't do what grown-ups wanted. But in the meantime things have changed. In most European countries it is now forbidden by law to beat your children. I can understand that some situations in life are not exactly easy to handle. And if parents are stressed and off their nerves, they might happen to slap a child in a specific setting. It's not good if it happens, but it's human. What irritates me is that you feel so totally self-assured about exercising physical discipline.

My husband also used to beat my son when he was little. And you know how I stopped this? I photographed my son's bruises and brought the pictures to a friend. Just to make sure that he couldn't destroy them. And then I told my spouse if he should ever do this again, I would report it to the police.

So be happy that I am not around!

Linda

20th of April 2012
Hi Linda,

You are so self-righteous!
And you understand nothing at all!
From what you have told me, your husband strongly disliked his stepson. And if such a man beats a child, he just does so because he wants to get rid of his anger.
How can you compare this to me and my daughter?! I love my daughter, and I would never do anything that isn't good for her. But love doesn't mean that you spoil your children. The bible teaches us that it is even necessary to spank them because only that way they will learn to discern right from wrong and grow up to be valuable members of society. And as a parent I should not beat my children because I am drunk, for example. This would be an abuse of the parental dominance that is given to me by God. Apart from this, in my country it is not forbidden to slap children. It is part of the parental rights to exer-

cise physical discipline in a responsible way. European countries are just stupid in some aspects. But you see what you get in return! A lot of young people who are totally out of control! Just look at your own daughter Kate! So far none of my children has set my house on fire! This all just happened because your daughter had already developed a habit of disrespect. That's why she didn't listen when you warned her about this candle. The rest we know!! So in a way, it was maybe your fault! In my house something like that would never happen because I would have spanked her into obedience with my loving rod. A little spanking in time can rule out a lot of big future problems! It's pure luck or maybe the grace of God that your flat wasn't destroyed in that fire! And all of this happened just because you have failed to teach your children discipline!

Yours honestly,
Stephen

21st of April 2012
Hi Stephen,

I would have never thought that you could say something like this! As far as I know, you also have a grown-up son who isn't exactly behaving towards you in this wonderful, respectful way which you continuously refer to.

And of course, it's typical for religious people that they always hide behind the Bible. Don't you understand: The Bible was written in completely different times in order to control simple and primitive people who strolled around in the desert. All those instructions in the bible were designed for the actual living conditions of people in those biblical times. They might even have been modern then, but in the meantime things have changed! Human beings have developed and evolved. Not everything that is recommended in the bible makes sense if you apply it to our modern world!

Linda

22nd of April 2012
Hi Linda,

It's so typical! If you lack proper arguments, you just attack my faith!
You are wrong, WRONG, WRONG!!!
The bible is the word of God, and it is true always! As it was true in the past it is true now, and it will be true and valid for the future. The

word of God is the base of all truth for all times. I actually feel sorry for you because you don't have any decent Christian faith. I pray that someday you can still find the truth!!

Yours,
Stephen

24th of April 2012
Hi Stephen,

Oh yes! The truth!
There is no such thing as "The Truth". Every human being has its own truth.

And besides, if you are such a good Christian as you claim, why do you then kick a poor old man who is sitting on the street with your foot? From what I know, Jesus always had compassion when he saw such people! I didn't say anything when I saw you doing so in Accra, but it definitely irritated me.

Linda

25th of April 2012
Hi Linda,

You have no idea about those people. They are a threat to society, and this all has nothing to do with the compassion Jesus had on people. If such people accepted the Lord as their saviour, it would change their lives, and they wouldn't even be sitting there anymore. Those people are fraudsters, and you shouldn't support them. The wicked have to be banned from the earth, thus says the word of God! Just like those Nigerians. That's evil people. You just don't check it!

Steve

27th of April 2012
Hi Stephen,

I know that you hate Nigerians. But I have a client here in Vienna who is from Nigeria, and he is one of the most positive and radiant people I have ever seen. He is married to an Austrian woman, and he successfully managed to become a civil engineer. He has confirmed to me that the people of Nigeria and Ghana don't like each other. He has also told me that in the past people from Ghana had tried to get visas for England from Nigerian ground. Because Nigeria had special visa conditions. So they pretended migrating to Nigeria first and as soon as they became Nigerians, they immediately applied for a visa to Great Britain. At some point this practise was stopped, and Nigeria kicked them out. No more visas attained by fraud! That made them sour. They had to go back to Ghana with all their belongings packed into a few huge bags. You know, those big bags of cheap quality which you can fold up when they are empty and which you see everywhere in the world, are in Nigeria called "Ghana must go bag"! So maybe this mutual hatred between your nations doesn't derive only from the given fact that "Nigerians are evil".

Linda

28th of April 2012
Hi Linda,

It's really incredible that you believe some Nigerian that you meet in Vienna more than me. I think you just want to insult me! First you question my authority, next you attack my faith and now you believe the word of a Nigerian more than mine!

And I really believed that we could maybe have a future together. I am highly disappointed about you.

Stephen

2nd of May 2012
Dear Stephen,

I've been thinking about things a lot in the past days. I've read all of our recent mails again, and I also recapped the days in Accra.

Guess we were both basically aware that in such online contacts there are certain levels missing. Actually, once you meet in person, you have to start on ground zero again.
It can be so easy to fall in love with a person that is far away …
And I knew well that going to Accra probably meant to kill a dream.
I think it was wise in this situation to hold up the friendship aspect again. After all, true friendship is so much more reliable than the crazy escapades of the heart!

To be honest, the moment I first met you at the airport, I felt pretty lost. But then I quickly felt secure again within the reassuring frame of our declared friendship. And I told myself that after all it was totally normal that we both seemed a bit guarded at first because genuine closeness needs time.

It was definitely nice getting to know your town, and I want to thank you for all the time and trouble you invested to show me around. And I have to say that my hopes were still up when we went to that "Canopy Walk". Remember when you told me about your fear of heights on the phone? I promised to kiss you up there! And I sure wish that kissing you had been a more pleasant experience than it actually was! Come on, shouldn't you know yourself that when kissing a person for the first time, you have to be a little bit careful and considerate? And that your kiss should never ever hurt!!
I really don't know … maybe you are just kind of unskilled in handling a woman. But please, don't do that again, or I can promise you that every woman will back off.

And then, when we touched ground again after that walk, you didn't act like we had just shared our first kiss. You engaged in heavy conversation with those two American girls to the point that you didn't even realise that you banged your elbow several times into my face whilst gesticulating. Don't get me wrong: It's fine that you talk to them! But you still have to know where *I* am, at every single moment. How can I feel comfortable with a man who bumps into me all the time!?

And I told you before that I didn't like it how you kicked that old man with your foot or how you always voice this ridiculous hatred towards "Nigerians". All these things confounded me a lot even if I didn't say a word. But there comes a time when we have to give people a piece of our mind …

You know, when I went back to Austria, I was disappointed because by then I knew for sure that we have no potential to be lovers. But I focused on the friendship again which I still valued very much. And I was more than willing to keep my promise that we would be friends always, no matter what.

And it is not easy for me what I'm going to say now, but this issue about beating your daughter is something I just cannot deal with. The mere thought of it just totally horrifies me. It's not that I cannot understand if somebody loses his temper in a specific situation. But this attitude of executing physical punishment out of conviction is something I'm totally opposed to.

I know that you probably can't understand why this is such a big deal to me. I also realise that in your country this is a personal right, even backed up by law and religion.

But it reminds me too much of this past situation when my husband used to beat my son. And believe me, even if I had fallen in love with you, I could have never enjoyed your touch, knowing that with those same hands that you use to caress me, you also beat a child.

And now that I haven't even fallen in love with you, I just feel that I don't want to carry on this friendship. The promise I have given was to a person close to my heart that you have unfortunately turned out NOT TO BE.

Therefore I do not feel bound to it anymore.

Linda

3rd of May 2012

Well, Linda, I would have never ever thought that someday I could get such a rude letter from you. It is a total insult to my person and everything I believe in. And since you now finally admit that you don't like me, you feel free to criticise every little detail. I thought you were an understanding, tolerant person, but I guess I was mistaken. And I'll tell you something: You probably were never interested in me; you just like to travel and used me as a comfortable possibility to come to Accra.

And to someone like you, I have given my true, honest emotions!! Makes me feel like an idiot now!! But I should have known better! There will be a reason why you haven't been happy with any of your husbands for a long time. You just don't know what love is all about!!

Steve

5th of May 2012

Well, Steve, just to get this straight, I never had any wish to travel to Accra. I came there only to meet *you!* But I didn't get to see much of your world. I haven't met anybody from your family, which I can understand. But I haven't even been trusted to meet your dog. I just got to see tourist attractions …

Linda

6th of May 2012

How ridiculous can you get, Linda!
I mean, it's not so easy here to take a dog to another place. Besides, my son has misplaced the chain. But you could have said something if this really was so important to you!

Steve

7th of May 2012

It doesn't matter anymore, Steve!
It's all over!

2nd of June 2012
Dear Linda,

Have you overcome your negative feelings in the meantime, dear? I hope so. I just want to assure you that I didn't mean the offensive things I recently said. Besides, I'm truly sorry that I couldn't make you feel happy close to me. I'm afraid, you are right. I'm a physically strong man, and I should have been more considerate.

But I didn't intend to hurt you. I've always just wanted the best for the two of us.

And deep in my heart I suppose that you didn't really mean the nasty things you said. You were just upset and wanted to hurt me in that moment. Right!?

So, please!! Let's forget about that stupid fight!

Yours,
Stephen

3rd of June 2012
Dear Stephen,

I'm sorry about the situation but I can only say that I was serious about every word I said. Nevertheless, I wish you all the best.

Linda

30th of May 2015

My dearest Linda,

It's been three years by now that we haven't heard anything from each other. But I will never forget you, Linda!
I would also like to thank you so much for all your emotional support concerning the dream house. You have really encouraged me a lot.
In the meantime I have moved there, and it's just so lovely to enjoy it every day.

Congratulations to Cora's fifth birthday!
How is she?
I hope everybody is fine in your place.

Yours, always,
Stephen

1st of June 2015

Little Cora says "Thank you".
By now she is fine. But some months ago we almost lost her. She found a bone in the park and I let her take it home and eat it. I didn't know that small dogs cannot eat so much bone. That it can actually block their intestines to the point

that they can die from it. Well, that day in the evening Cora felt obviously lousy, and we consulted the animal clinic that night for advice. In the morning there was severe bleeding from her gut, and I rushed her to the clinic. They had to warm her up first until she was stable enough for the surgery. And then five days later she needed a second operation because a huge abscess had developed inside the wound. They didn't even have time to ask me for permission! Well, when she came back home after two weeks, she was really skinny and always hungry. But now she is all happy and healthy again. It would have been a shame if she had died at such an early age just because of a silly thing like this.

How is Penny?

Linda

4th of June 2015

Oh Linda,

I'm glad to hear that little Cora is fine.

Unfortunately Penny has died in a car accident. She ran across the street to follow my daughter who had just left to get some films from the video shop. Poor Penny was hit by a car and died the same day.

But maybe she has saved us from having an accident that way. You know, believe it or not, some animals can die for us. They give themselves as a sacrifice and can suffer our diseases or accidents instead of us.

Take good care of yourself, Linda!
Life is a precious thing, and it can be gone so quickly.

Yours,
Stephen

24th of May 2020
Dear Stephen,

I just wish to inform you that I sometimes get such weird e-mails that look as if they come from your mail address but then lead to all kinds of spam pages or links.

I guess that you haven't sent those mails. I'm just telling you because I think you wouldn't want to be connected with some of those pages.

Hope you are doing fine in Ghana.

We had here a rather strict lockdown due to corona virus. From the 16th of March until the 2nd of May we were practically forbidden to leave the house, and I couldn't work for six weeks.

I realise that this is all a chain reaction because not only the richer countries, which can bail out their citizens, suffer. No, also in third world countries they are missing out. Airplanes have no travellers, hotels have no tourists, and even the little people who sell their handmade souvenirs, lose their income.

This virus just affects everybody somehow!

Please confirm having received my message. I've tried to contact you about those mails before, but somehow I could never get in touch.

Linda

31ˢᵗ of August 2020
Hello Linda, my dear,

Thanks for telling me about the inappropriate use of my e-mail address. I also sometimes get such weird mails, seems to be a common practice these days …

For a long time I wondered why I never got any response to my last mail which I sent you five years ago …

And guess what …? Just this moment I have found your message in the spam box after waiting for so long to hear from you!!
By the way, only a few days later your mail would have been lost due to the automatic delete function!!

We also have restrictions because of Covid 19, like social distancing, intensified hygiene and masks. But luckily it hasn't been too bad so far since our infection numbers are relatively low.

I no longer log into that internet platform where we met so long ago. I left you some messages there from time to time but eventually realised that you haven't been there in ages. Was truly worried about you, but at some point I calmed down, thinking that you might have gone on a long journey ...

Please let me know how you are doing. I'm very fine myself, just that I've missed you so much ...

Hugs and kisses
Stephen